The Good Luck Sister

Also by Jill Shalvis

Women's Fiction Novels
Lost and Found Sisters
The Good Luck Sister (novella)

Coming Soon
Rainy Day Friends

Heartbreaker Bay Novels
About That Kiss
Chasing Christmas Eve
Accidentally on Purpose
The Trouble with Mistletoe
Sweet Little Lies

Lucky Harbor Novels
One in a Million
He's So Fine
It's in His Kiss
Once in a Lifetime
Always on My Mind

The Good Luck Sister

A WILDSTONE NOVELLA

JILL SHALVIS

WILLIAM MORROW IMPULSE

An Imprint of HarperCollinsPublishers

*For all the wonderful readers of LOST AND
FOUND SISTERS who wrote me that they just
couldn't let Tilly and Dylan go, that they needed
their story. This one is for you . . . XOXO, Jill*

Excerpt from *Rainy Day Friends* copyright © 2018 by Jill Shalvis.

THE GOOD LUCK SISTER. Copyright © 2018 by Jill Shalvis. All rights reserved. Printed in the United States of America. No part of this book may be used or reproduced in any manner whatsoever without written permission except in the case of brief quotations embodied in critical articles and reviews. For information, address HarperCollins Publishers, 195 Broadway, New York, NY 10007.

Digital Edition MAY 2018 ISBN: 978-0-06246359-3
Print Edition ISBN: 978-0-06246361-6

Cover design by Nadine Badalaty
*Cover photographs © Cynthia Kidwell/Shutterstock (dog); © fotohunter/
Shutterstock(Sky); © fotohunter/ shutterstock (picnic basket and blanket);
© Tomas Zrna/ Getty Images (landscape)*

William Morrow Impulse is a trademark of HarperCollins Publishers.

William Morrow and HarperCollins are registered trademarks of HarperCollins Publishers in the United States of America and other countries.

FIRST EDITION

18 19 20 21 22   HDC   10 9 8 7 6 5 4 3 2

Acknowledgments

To COOP THE POOP, who was the inspiration for Leo and also a failed foster pup turned forever fur baby by my oldest daughter. :)

Chapter 1

I've finished my free trial of adulthood and am no longer interested, so please cancel my subscription.

—from "The Mixed-Up Files of Tilly Adams's Journal"

TILLY ADAMS SAT in the vet's office staring at the doctor in shock. "Say that again?"

Dr. Janet Lyons smiled. "I think Leo faked being sick. Probably so you'd stay home from work today."

Tilly looked down at Leo. "You do know he's a dog, right?"

All six pounds of him smiled up at her. About a month ago, she found him on a street corner hiding beneath a bus bench; wet, dirty, cold, hungry and matted.

He'd been Dobby meets Gremlin meets neglected, abused Care Bear. Tilly had looked around for an adult, and then had to remind herself that at twenty-five years old, she was legal herself. So then she'd searched for an adultier adult, but she'd been the only one in sight.

So she'd scooped the little guy up and had brought him to the SPCA, who'd said he was about five weeks old, a possible Maltipoo, which meant he came by his Care Bear look naturally. He was malnutritioned and suffering from mange. They'd said they'd do what they could, and Tilly had turned to go. That had been when she'd seen all the eyes on her from an endless row of cages . . . and she'd realized her Care Bear would soon be sitting in one too. Then she'd heard herself offer to foster him until they found him a forever home.

They'd found him one too. Tilly had signed the adoption papers last weekend in spite of the fact that just that morning he'd escaped his crate, eaten her favorite sneakers, destroyed her favorite pillow, and then yakked up the stuffing from the pillow.

He was a destructo of the highest magnitude, and something else too. He had no idea how small he was. He went after her sister Quinn's twenty-plus pound cat and her neighbor's hundred pound black lab with the same fierce, fearless gusto. Turned out, the little guy had a bad case of small-man syndrome, which was how he'd earned his name.

Leo, short for Napoleon.

And now on top of Leo's impressive chewing skills,

his escape artist skills, and his ability to get up on her bed and yet still not understand why stepping in his own poop was annoying, he had a new skill.

He'd faked being sick.

Proud of himself, Leo smiled up at her. Smiled. An hour ago he'd been coughing and limping and acting all sorts of odd. Now he just kept smiling up at her while sending her meaningful glances at the open dog biscuit bin between her and the doctor.

Dr. Lyons laughed and gave him one.

"Dogs can't fake sick," Tilly said while Leo inhaled the biscuit whole before licking the floor to make sure he got all the crumbs. "Can they?"

Dr. Lyons scooped him up and gave him a kiss on his adorable snout. "Yours did."

Tilly sighed. It was too early for this. She'd had a crazy late night. Not hanging at Whiskey River, the local bar and grill. Not at a club with friends. Not working on her designs for the upcoming graphic art showing.

Nope, she'd been on a serious stress bender—a marathon of *Game of Thrones*. She hadn't fallen asleep until after two and her alarm had interrupted her in the middle of a really great dream starring Jon Snow.

Dr. Lyons handed Leo over. He immediately snuggled into the crook of Tilly's neck and dammit, her cold heart melted on the spot and she hugged him close. "You're sure he's okay? He was coughing. And then he limped funny. And then he wouldn't eat."

"But he hasn't coughed once that I've seen. And he's

not limping either. And you said all his food vanished while you took a quick shower."

"Yes," Tilly said.

Dr. Lyons waited for her to catch up.

Tilly sighed. "He really did fake me out."

"You mentioned you've been working long hours in the studio, right? And also taking extra shifts at Caro's Café. And now you're teaching art at the community college as well. I think Leo's lonely. Take him to work with you today and see what happens."

"It's my first day teaching."

The vet smiled. "He'll warm up your students for you."

That, or eat their shoes. Tilly sighed and put Leo in his little carrier bag that doubled as her purse. She paid the office visit tab with her already loaded credit card, and got in her car.

Wildstone was a small California coastal and ranching town that sat in a bowl between the Pacific Coast and wine country. She'd grown up here, a wild child who favored riding her bike through the oak-covered rolling hills or hiding in the bluffs above the ocean to school work and social niceties. She'd been raised by her mom until she'd passed away when Tilly had been fifteen. Her older sister, Quinn, had come to live with her and took over parental duties.

Tilly hadn't been exactly welcoming. In fact, she'd been a nightmare. She'd thought she'd been so original, but the truth was, she'd been a classic cliché, ignoring curfew, sneaking out, "borrowing" the car and then crashing it . . . but somehow she and Quinn had fumbled their way through.

And Tilly had gone on to become an adult, as dubious as that seemed at the moment as she raced to school with a foster fail puppy in her purse. She'd come back to Wildstone after graduating college a few years ago. She'd had a few stints at the local art fairs, but nothing had come of them and she'd gotten her teaching credential to pay the bills. Somehow in the doing of that, she realized she'd given up the big artist dream in order to have a roof over her head and food in her belly.

"You'll be a good art teacher," she told herself and looked over at Leo. "Right?"

"Arf!"

Right. She'd get to impart her knowledge. She'd be content. She would.

She parked at the community college and stared at the busy place. She'd be here every Monday, Wednesday, and Friday, teaching three classes on each of those days. Blowing out a sigh, she texted her sister.

Tilly: How you doing?

Quinn: I'm thirty months pregnant, how do you think I'm doing? I'm peeing every two seconds and eating the house. Why aren't you here dropping Leo off?

Tilly: Thanks for offering to pup-sit, but I'm bringing him with me.

Quinn: Are you nuts?

Tilly: Yes. And also feeling guilty. I just signed the adoption papers yesterday. It's too early to foist him off on someone.

Quinn: Aw, look at you being a good dog mom. Just don't look directly into his soft brown eyes. Trust me, he'll mind meld you into doing whatever he wants. It's a fatal flaw. Good luck. You're going to need it.

No doubt. She got out of the car and headed to her classroom, her purse over one shoulder with Leo's head out bouncing with her every step, his tongue lolling happily at the sights.

"Arf!" he said in an excited bark so high it was almost inaudible.

Tilly tried to catch some of his enthusiasm, and clutching her things, kept moving.

It was going to be a day of firsts. First day of the week. First day of teaching. First day of skipping breakfast thanks to the nerves of first day of teaching.

And first day of being speechless as a few minutes later, with Leo now asleep in her bag, standing in front of her students, specifically the guy sitting front and center.

At the sight of him, time stuttered to a halt. So did the breath in her lungs. She had to be seeing things. Stress induced, exhaustion induced, lack of sugar induced . . . Whatever the reason, she fumbled for her glasses in the front pocket of her portfolio and slid them on. Pushing them up her nose, she took another peek.

But nope, he was still sitting there, the unwelcome blast from her past, his dark eyes taking her in, expression hooded and unreadable.

Her heart kicked hard and she began to sweat. She pulled out her iPad and accessed her class roster, the one she hadn't had a chance to look at since receiving it late last night. She took a look at the list and froze.

Dylan Scott was listed. He'd registered for her class.

She jerked her gaze back up. His mouth curved slightly and she lost concentration. Quickly, she mentally ran through her tricks for her public speaking anxiety. *Don't look them right in the eyes. Look just over their heads. Smile. Breathe. Repeat.*

Don't stroke out.

"Hello, everyone," she said with more cheer than she felt. Because what she felt was the urge to run home, dive under her covers, and stay there until the semester was over. Nerves jangling in her stomach, she forced a smile. "Welcome to Graphic Design 101."

She got a few murmurs. A very few. Still doing her best to ignore Dylan in the front row—and failing spectacularly—she tried not to be bummed at the low level of enthusiasm. It was eight A.M., she reminded herself. And a Monday. Plus, this class was an elective, which meant people took it as a filler and *not* because they were excited about learning graphic art.

"It's going to be fun," she said as cheerfully as she could while also squirming just a little bit under the dark, speculative gaze of Dylan.

Why hadn't she taken more care with her hair? And had she even put on a lick of makeup? She couldn't remember. "Really," she said. "I promise." She tried to think of her next line, but her brain was on repeat. Dylan. Dylan. Dylan . . . "I'm sorry," she finally said and looked right at him. "But why are you here?"

Everyone risked whiplash trying to get a glimpse of who she was speaking to. There were whispers and a few nervous giggles.

Dylan didn't look bothered in the least. He didn't fidget. Didn't even blink. "Wanted to learn graphic design," he said.

Bullshit. When they'd first met, he'd been sixteen to her fifteen and he'd had not a single artistic inkling. He'd wanted to be an astronaut.

She'd wanted to be a world-famous artist. Only she hadn't gotten even close. That she had that upcoming show at the art gallery downtown was in thanks to Quinn and Mick for donating heavily. But she'd figured a pity show was better than no show at all.

As for Dylan, she knew from a few late night, alcohol fueled online searches that she wouldn't admit to even under the threat of death that he'd gone into the marines. He'd made something of himself.

And she'd been swimming in place.

From the podium, her phone flashed a Twitter notification.

Day One, Teacher @TillyAdams is losing her shit in art class. Going to be fun . . .

Perfect. "If you'll all excuse us a minute," she said to the class and gestured for Dylan to meet her off to the side of the room.

With an easy, almost animalistic grace he rose from his chair and headed toward her while she did her best not to drown in memories. He was still long-legged and lanky, but filled out in all the right places, looking like the hottest thing she'd ever seen. But seriously, he had a lot of nerve showing up after all this time with zero contact after breaking her heart and crushing her soul. Good thing she was no longer a naive teenager. She had her life together. Completely. One hundred percent. Okay, sixty-five percent.

"I don't know what game you're playing," she whispered. "But it isn't funny. I think you should leave."

"No game," he said. "I'm signed up for this class, same as everyone else." And with that, he went back to his seat.

She looked around, felt the awkwardness of the room. Her doing. She was an idiot. She did her best to shake it off, to completely ignore him. Pride dictated this. All the anger, hurt, confusion, and the hardest to take, betrayal, she'd shoved deep eight years ago and nothing could get to that. Nothing.

As she began to go through the curriculum with the class, she walked around the large art room, showing them the wide variety of equipment they had at their fingertips thanks to a recent grant. They had large monitors at twenty stations, but the 3D printer was her favorite, and she quickly sketched out some blocks, showing the students how they might use the printer as a part of an upcoming 3D project. She put letters on the blocks to spell B-I-T-E M-E, realized what she was doing and the scrambled the letters before hitting print.

But not in time apparently, because the blocks came out in perfect order. "Well," she said. "It is a Monday, right?"

The class was cracking up and she took a discreet glance at Dylan.

He arched a brow.

She looked at the clock. Ten minutes had gone by. Forty more minutes to go.

When the bell finally rang and the students all began to exit the room, she turned away so she didn't feel tempted to watch Dylan leave.

The ratfink bastard.

She busied herself putting her things back into her bag and checked on Leo. The little guy yawned so sweetly and smiled sleepily up at her, melting her heart.

Scooping him up, she cuddled him to her, giving him a kiss on his snout. He smiled back and . . .

. . . Let loose with a warm stream. She felt it pool at her chest before dripping down her torso. Sucking in a breath, she pulled the pup away from her with a sigh.

He bicycled his little paws in the air, trying to get back to her, a smile on that deceptively adorable face.

"Okay," she said. "I'm willing to concede that was entirely my fault. Let's get you outside before this turns into a número dos situation." She turned to go and came face to face with Dylan. "*Dammit.*"

He looked amused at her greeting. His gaze ran over her, caught onto the puppy, and he gave Tilly a small smile. "Cute," he said, reaching out a hand to pet Leo.

Who bared his little teeth and gave a ferocious growl.

Okay, so it wasn't ferocious, it was thin and wobbly, like he wasn't quite sure how to growl, but he bared his teeth to show he meant it. Tilly was so stunned that she let out a startled laugh. Clearly she'd projected her feelings onto the pup. "Good boy," she said. Shouldering her purse and grabbing the portfolio, she lifted her chin in the air and started to walk away.

"Not going to even say hi?" Dylan asked her back.

She had to close her eyes for a beat because of that voice. Once upon a time, that sexy, gruff voice could stop her in her tracks. She'd always known that, thanks to a tragically rough childhood, he had inner demons. But she'd always thought they'd fight them together.

He'd lied about that. He'd lied about a lot of things. "I have a *different* word for you," she said. "It's *good-bye*." And with as much dignity as she could manage while dripping puppy pee down her shirt and pants legs, she did as he'd once done to her. Walked away.

Chapter 2

"Of all her childhood memories, her favorite was never having to pay bills."

—from "The Mixed-Up Files of Tilly Adams's Journal"

Ten years prior:

TILLY SIGHED AND tossed and turned some more, stilling at a sudden ping of a rock on her window. Before she could get up, the window slid open and Dylan's long, lanky body climbed in.

Her best friend in the entire world had a fat lip and a black eye.

"I told you to keep this locked," he said. He was pissed.

And hurt.

Tilly drew him down to her bed to take care of him, like she did every time his asshole dad beat on him. She cupped his face, her eyes filling when she saw what had been done to him this time. "I want to kill him," she whispered.

"Shh," he said and closed his eyes. "If he touches my mom again, I'll kill him myself."

Fear for him made her legs wobble. His dad didn't live with Dylan and his mom, he'd been kicked out of the house several years back and now lived two towns over from Wildstone in Paso Robles. Whenever he came to "visit"—aka steal money from Dylan's mom—Dylan did his best to draw his attention away from her.

Brave. And terrifying.

Tilly got up and tiptoed into the kitchen where she grabbed an ice pack, and then on second thought also peanut butter and jelly, before heading back to her room.

Dylan hadn't moved.

He was a year older than she was, a grade ahead of her, and on a different planet when it came to life experiences. He ran with a fast crowd and wouldn't let her hang with them.

"You still have a shot at a good life," he always said when she asked. "I'm not going to fuck it up for you."

She sat crossed-legged on the bed at his side and gently laid the ice pack over his eye.

He hissed in a breath and she set a hand on his chest. He remained still, but the steady beat of his heart reassured her. And something else, something that was her own little secret.

Whenever she was close to him like this, she felt warm. Hot, even. And tight, like her skin had shrunk and her body didn't fit inside it.

She sighed, hating this big, fat crush she had on him.

If he knew, he'd vanish from her life, so she kept her damn infatuation to herself. "Hungry?"

Eyes still closed, his lips curved. "Always."

She laughed a little. This wasn't a lie, the guy was truly always starving, like he was hollow on the inside and nothing could fill him up.

She reached across Dylan for the pack of crackers she had on her nightstand. Her arm brushed his and she felt a tingle make its way through her body. "Here," she said, dipping the cracker first into the peanut butter and then the jelly, and holding it out to him.

He opened his eyes and then smiled. "PB and J for dinner."

"Is there anything better?"

"No." He sat up gingerly enough that she worried he'd been hurt elsewhere as well, but when he saw the look on her face, his eyes went dark. "Don't," he said and took the cracker, shoving the whole thing in his mouth.

"But—"

"Not talking about it, Tee."

They dipped crackers into the peanut butter and jelly until they were both full. Actually, she got full right away, but she didn't want him to stop until he was full as well, so she totally overate.

And then had to open the top button on her jeans.

After, Dylan pulled her down with him to the bed again and closed his eyes. She thought that she couldn't think of another place she'd rather be. She wanted them to grow up and still do this, still be like this. She'd be an artist and he'd be . . . "Dylan?" she whispered.

"Yeah?"

"What do you want to be when you get older?"

"Alive."

Her heart pinched. "I mean as a job."

His hand squeezed hers. "It doesn't matter," he said a little dully.

She knew what that meant. He didn't see himself making it out, and that made her so sad that she couldn't speak for a long moment.

As if he knew he'd brought her down, he stirred himself and changed the subject. "Did you finish your biology homework?"

"Shh," she said. "I'm sleeping."

"Tee."

"You can help me tomorrow," she murmured softly, letting herself relax against him, purposely letting him think she was exhausted.

She felt when the tension finally left him and he fell asleep. Only then did she allow her eyes to close. She was comfortable and she should've been thrilled because she never slept as well as she did when he was in her bed. But worry for him kept her up long after he'd drifted off . . .

On Wednesday, Dylan got to day two of graphic arts early, this time waiting for Tilly in the parking lot. After yesterday, he'd realized that surprising her in front of other people had been a tactical error. At the time, he'd thought seeing her in a public place might be easier for her. No, that was a lie. He'd been protecting himself.

He'd been wrong.

For a long time, he'd been aware that someday his mistakes would catch up with him and he'd pay. There'd been so many he also knew it was going to hurt.

Pain had been a way of life for him growing up, so there'd been no reason it should change now, but this pain was different because it was pain he'd caused in someone else, in Tilly of all people, the only person who'd ever been there for him through thick and thin.

There'd been a hell of a lot of thin in those days.

And as Tilly pulled into the lot, parked, and got out of her car and caught sight of him, he could see the pain he'd caused her etched in every line of her tense body. Her big baby blue eyes, and all the emotions in them, sliced him open.

He should've left well enough alone. And maybe those words would be on his gravestone, but for now he had to see this through.

Shaking her head, she gathered her things and started toward the campus. He reached out to stop her and the little dog in her purse went apeshit.

"Arf, arf, arf, ARF!"

"Leo," Tilly admonished. "Stop."

"Arf, arf, arf, ARF!"

And since this was accompanied by a show of teeth,

Dylan pulled his hand back, surprised because dogs loved him. "Tilly—"

"No," she said, and then as if she'd been holding it all in, the words burst from her like a tidal wave as she whirled back to face him. "I mean you just up and vanished on me after graduation! You said you were going off to think, which implied you'd be back. You didn't come back, Dylan, you went into the military, which is the opposite of coming back!"

He never took his dark gaze off hers. "I know."

She shook her head. "You were my best friend and the love of my life, and you never even looked back. You're such an asshole."

"I know," he repeated. "And I didn't mean to throw you by taking your class. I just . . ."

"What?"

"Wanted to see you."

She shook her head, like she didn't believe him, not that he could blame her. "Drop the class," she said. "We have nothing more to discuss."

He knew that was the smart thing to do. He shouldn't have come to see her, but he was back in town now for the foreseeable future and hadn't wanted her to hear about it from anyone but him. When he'd learned she was teaching art at the community college, he'd been so proud. Art had always been her dream and she was making it come true for herself. But no amount of internet searching could tell him the one thing he needed to know more than anything else. Was she happy? So he'd had to come see her in her element. "How about business?" he said. "I hear you're a pretty fantastic graphic artist. I'm starting up a helicopter touring company with two buddies. Wildstone Air Tours. We need a logo."

She turned away.

"I'm paying," he said.

She froze and then slowly turned back to him. And just as it'd been yesterday at the first sight of her, it was like being punched in the gut.

In high school, she'd been skinny, favored all black clothing, and had an attitude to match.

She was no longer skin and bones, having filled out in all the right places. There wasn't an ounce of black on her anywhere, but her attitude was still there and made him want to smile.

"Are you thinking about laughing at me?" she asked in disbelief.

"I wouldn't dare. Are you interested in the work?"

"I'm angry, not stupid," she said. "I'll think about it."

"Ball's in your court."

She nodded and . . . didn't move away.

Ridiculously eager to make the moment last, he took a step closer, keeping one eye on the dog. "Vicious guard dog," he said. "All what, four pounds of him?"

"Six pounds."

Dylan eyed him. "If you say so." He looked into Tilly's eyes. "It's good to see you."

"Is it?"

"Yes. Very."

She shook her head and turned away. "I'm going now. I'd say don't call me, but that'd be a waste of breath since you won't call anyway."

He deserved that and a whole lot more.

Which didn't explain the very rusty-feeling smile on his face.

THAT AFTERNOON, DYLAN stood in the center of the hangar in the small airport just outside of Wildstone, staring at the new big sign that read: WILDSTONE AIR TOURS. Just looking at it and the two helicopters in front of him had an unaccustomed feeling settling in his chest. *Tentative excitement.* Tentative, because things like hope and joy had been rare commodities in his life.

"We did it, man," Penn said, coming up to his side and clapping him on the back. "From the suckage of boot camp to the suckage of Afghanistan to the suckage of South America, we pulled ourselves out of the ditches to become our own bosses, just like we always wanted."

"Yeah." Dylan shook his head. "Hard to believe."

"No, what's hard to believe is that our lives are finally going to be ours again. We might actually get some semblance of . . . normal."

Dylan had to laugh. He'd grown up with a drunk of a father who de-stressed by beating on his family. Penn didn't know his dad and his mom had taken off on him when he'd been young. "What do either of us know about being normal?"

"Good point," Penn said with a shrug. "But it's going to be fun to try, right?" He grinned. "Know what I'm going to do first?"

"Get laid?" Ric, their third musketeer, strode into the hangar.

"Yes!" Penn said. "*That.* It's been way too long."

"It's been a week," Dylan said dryly. "The walls in our new place are way too thin and she *really* liked your name."

Penn grinned. "You're just jealous because you haven't had anyone like screaming your name in . . ." He looked at Ric. "Jeez, when was the last time our boy got some?"

"He's definitely due," Ric said.

"We don't have time for that," Dylan said. Not if they were going to make this work. He was pilot and business manager. Penn was pilot number two and their entire sales department—the guy could sell a whorehouse to a nun. Ric was the money guy. He'd come from money and tended to turn shit into gold. Together they held the lease on this hangar—which they'd been given a deal on through a contact of Ric's. And by deal, he meant steal. They had a gratifying amount of new business clients interested. Giving tours for the local wineries. Tourist traffic at the beaches. And some taxiing of high profile clients back and forth from Santa Barbara, Los Angeles, and San Francisco.

If only half of it came to fruition, they might actually make it.

"There's always time for the fairer sex," Penn said.

"Or not the fairer sex," Ric said. He'd broken off a longtime relationship with his last boyfriend about six months ago for cheating on him and was finally out of the dumps.

"No," Dylan said. "Business first. We've got to get—" He broke off when someone else came into the hangar.

The three of them turned in tandem, surprised at the sound of heels click, click, clicking across the concrete floor. Feminine steps. The setting sun slashing in the doorway made it difficult to see beyond a curvy figure and . . . a tiny little rat on a leash. Hold up. Not a rat.

A gremlin.

Tilly's gremlin.

"Excuse me," she said, shielding her eyes, clearly not able to see them any more clearly than she could see them. "I'm looking for Dylan Scott."

Ric and Penn simultaneously elbowed Dylan in the sides, like maybe he was unaware of his own name. Shaking his head at them, he stepped forward out of the shadow.

The rat—er, her dog, starting yipping at the sight of him. With a sigh, he crouched down to the thing and looked him in the eyes. "Are we going to do this every time?"

"Arf, arf, *ARF*!"

Yep, they were. He held out his fist. The pup sniffed it and seemed to accept this as a peace offering. Relieved at the silence, Dylan rose to his feet and looked at Tilly.

Who was suddenly looking very slightly less hostile, he thought. But that might have been wishful thinking. "Hey," he said. "What are you doing here?"

"I looked up Wildstone Air Tours and got this address. I wanted to talk to you." Her eyes slid to the two men just behind him and she lowered her voice. "Business only."

"Got it," he said, willing to take whatever he could get. For now.

Penn came up to Dylan's side, slinging an arm around his neck. "We were hoping our boy here had a woman tucked away in his hometown. But business is even better."

At the "woman tucked away in his hometown" Tilly narrowed her eyes at Dylan.

Shaking his head at Penn, he spoke directly to Tilly. "This idiot is actually one of my partners. Penn." He pointed to Ric. "And Ric here is another partner, and our CFO." He looked at the guys. "This is Tilly Adams."

Both guys went brows up at the sound of her name. They'd been together long enough for them to know the whole story, but thankfully Penn kept his trap shut. They each shook Tilly's hand.

"If this guy gives you any trouble though," Penn told her, "you be sure to let me know."

She laughed but got serious when they left. She'd changed out of her teacher clothes for a lightweight, loose halter top over cropped jeans that fit her like a glove. She'd added a pair of wedge sandals, giving her a few extra inches on her five two frame, something he knew she did when she felt she needed extra confidence.

That she felt that with him was his own damn fault.

"Give me a tour?" she asked.

"Sure." He led her around the hangar, showing her their pride and joy, their fleet of two helicopters that both he and Penn would fly as often as they could, a Bell 206 and an AStar 350.

"Wow," Tilly whispered reverently, running a hand along the body of the Bell. "You really fly these?"

"Yeah."

"It's amazing, Dylan." She turned from the chopper to face him, her eyes searching his. He wondered what she saw when she looked at him like that, and knew at least part of her couldn't help but see him as that sixteen-year-old kid who climbed in her window bleeding and hurting at night after his dad had beat on him.

He hated that to the very depths of his soul.

"You did it," she murmured. "You got out and made something of yourself."

It was a reminder that at one time she'd known him better than anyone else ever had. "It's not like I became an astronaut."

Something shuttered in her eyes at that. "Yeah, well, life happens, right? Shit happens."

He stepped toward her but she shook her head. It wasn't Leo's low growl that stopped him but Tilly's expression. "I just came by to tell you that I'd give your branding a shot," she said and pulled a card from her purse with her name and contact information. "Send me what you need. Specs. Ideas. Inspirations. Whatever you've got. I'll get back to you within a week."

"Tilly—"

She shook her head. "Business only," she said, repeating her earlier words, and then was gone.

Chapter 3

Mondays should be optional.

—from "The Mixed-Up Files of
Tilly Adams's Journal"

Ten years prior:

WHEN DYLAN MISSED class for the third day in a row, Tilly went to his mom's house first. When the woman answered the door, she told Tilly that Dylan had just left.

Tilly's gaze strayed to his mom's fat lip.

"Not Dylan's doing," she told Tilly softly, tears in her voice.

Which meant that Dylan's dad had been here and there'd been another fight. She froze, remembering what Dylan had promised the last time—that he'd kill the guy if he laid another finger on his mom.

Panic nearly choked her.

Ten minutes later she was on a bus heading toward Dylan's dad's house, the address written on a piece of paper clutched in her hand. Half an hour later, she stood in front of a small ranch house. It was run-down, but there was a lot of acreage. She could smell cattle and hear mooing off in the distance.

The house wasn't close to any others, which didn't feel like a good thing. Yelling was coming from inside, and then the sounds of something crashing and breaking, and she ran to the front door.

It was locked.

Heart racing, she pounded on it. "Dylan!"

No answer. But she could still hear shouting inside, so she hurried around the side of the house to the back. There was a patio and a slider, which slid right open under her hand. She stepped into a living room, lit only by the spill of lights from a bedroom down the hall, from which the sounds of a fight drew her.

Heart lodged in her throat, she looked around for something to protect herself with. Nothing. She glanced down at her hands and realized she was still clutching the soda bottle she'd bought while waiting for her bus.

The hallway ended all too fast and then she stood in the doorway of a bedroom. Dylan was in the corner, down like he'd just fallen, blood coming from his nose and mouth, one eye swollen nearly shut, shirt ripped, watching a man twice his size come at him.

THE FOLLOWING MONDAY, Tilly watched Dylan walk into her classroom and she couldn't even say she was surprised. He'd once been the most stubborn person on the planet and apparently not much had changed there.

He sat in the front row again. On one side of him was a surfer stoner. "Dude," the guy said. "Think she's going to tell you to bite her again?"

The girl on the other side of Dylan smiled at him. "You can bite me if you'd like."

Oh for God's sake, Tilly thought. And yet . . . a small part of her could admit that getting her mouth on him would be . . . extremely satisfying.

Ignoring the thought *and* Dylan, she concentrated on the class plan, which involved incorporating traditional sketching into graphic art. Because she believed that the two went hand in hand, they were starting with a basic drawing lesson. She had all her students sketching a bowl of fruit that was on display in the center of the room in the lap of a male model who was posed eating an apple.

The model was Mason, a good friend and sort of ex, who was in need of work and doing Tilly a favor. She walked around the class speaking to her students about technique, all of which appeared to be going over the head of the one student she'd really hoped wouldn't show up.

Dylan. She'd stayed up late last night working on logos and branding for Wildstone Air Tours and had emailed him everything this morning to avoid the face to face. She realized he was watching her watch him and with a sigh, headed over there. "Problem?"

"I can't draw," he admitted.

She looked at his paper. The apple was there. That

was it. "Maybe it's because you're staring at me instead of listening."

"I'm staring because today you look so much like sixteen-year -old Tilly, it's making me crazy."

When he said stuff like that, she had to close her eyes and take a breath. She was wearing a black cotton sundress that was modest and comfortable, but she could admit it might be a throwback to her emo days. Her white beat-up sneakers were speckled with paint, but too perfectly worn in to toss. So yeah, okay, maybe she looked sixteen . . . "I'm not that same Tilly," she said.

He nodded. "I'm getting that."

"Are you? Because I told you not to come back and yet here you are."

"I got your email with the logo and branding," he said. "You nailed it and I wanted to thank you."

This gave her a flash of relief and pleasure. "Now see, that's something where you could have hit reply and emailed instead of telling me in person. Especially since we decided this was going to be business only."

"Actually," he said, "that was you. I haven't decided any such thing."

The class was filled with whispers now. Some "oohs" and "ahhs" and a teasing "teacher's gotta pet." One of the girls muttered, "I wouldn't kick him out of bed for eating crackers . . ."

"Me either," a guy said.

"Come on, Ms. Adams," someone called out. "Give him a chance. It gives the rest of us hope."

Tilly made a show of glancing at the clock on the wall and the students settled.

At the end of class, Dylan managed to dawdle until it was just the two of them in the room.

"Where's Leo today?" he asked.

"My niece is watching him." She'd hoped to avoid getting peed on at work.

He nodded. "Art's not my strong suit," he said showing her his rather pathetic stick figure drawing.

"I don't get it," she said. "I don't get why you don't just stay away from me. You managed to do it for all those years, so why are you having trouble doing it now?"

"That question's above my pay grade."

She rolled her eyes.

"Okay, fine," he said and shrugged. "I can't seem to help myself."

She stared at him. "Don't even try to tell me that after you left town without saying good-bye you pined away for me."

"I didn't."

Okay, ouch.

"I'm telling you I moved you out of my heart so I could function," he said.

She took a beat to process that. "Did you . . . 'function' with other women?"

He didn't look away. Instead he held eye contact with no sign that this conversation was as uncomfortable for him as it was for her. "It's been eight years since we were together, Tee."

Tee. His childhood nickname for her. She knew it'd rolled off his tongue without him even thinking about it, that it didn't mean anything, but it made her ache. "So yes, you did."

"As did you."

Their gazes held and bunches of unwanted and unwelcome longing and nostalgia welled up inside her, damn him. When he'd been in her life, she'd been . . . well, a mess. After her mom's death, she'd learned she'd had a sister she hadn't known about, Quinn, who'd willingly stepped in to be her guardian, and it'd been the most anxiety-ridden, stressful, traumatic time of her life. The only reason she'd gotten through any of it was because of Dylan. But he'd left her.

And now he was in Wildstone.

Good thing she was no longer a lost teenager in need of an anchor.

"Thanks again for the logo and branding," he said quietly. He pulled out a check that matched the invoice she'd attached to the email.

She slipped it into her pocket. "Thanks for the work."

"Tee—"

"I've got to go," she said.

He held her gaze for a long beat, nodded, and then let her be as she'd wanted—alone.

THE NEXT DAY, Dylan got up before dawn, took a long, hard, fast run to try and outpace his demons.

He couldn't.

For breakfast, he stopped at Caro's, the café Quinn and Tilly had inherited from their mom. Quinn was in the kitchen, but not cooking. She was sitting huge belly up to a table slicing carrots.

"Still trying to make us all eat healthy?" he asked from the doorway.

She looked up and smiled. "I was hoping you'd come by and say hi. Let me look at you." Her critical eye swept over him. "You don't look worse for wear on the outside." She met his gaze. "I'm assuming all the scars are on the inside?"

"Maybe I don't have any."

She snorted. "If that were true, you'd have been back in Wildstone a few years ago instead of taking all those skills Uncle Sam drilled into you to South America to pilot for hire." She let her smile fade. "I knew you were coming back a few weeks ago when you emailed Mick for an attorney recommendation to write up your new partnership agreement."

"You didn't tell Tilly," he said.

"I didn't," she said. "But make no mistake. I'm livid with you. You broke her heart and nearly destroyed her."

"I had to go," he said quietly. "We both know she would never have taken her scholarship, she'd have stayed here to be with me. She deserved better, Quinn, far better."

She stared at him for a long beat and then nodded. "I figured. And I didn't tell her you were coming back because I didn't want to mess her all up if it turned out to not be true. I loved and adored you, still do, but my loyalty is with her, always."

He nodded. "I get that."

"Do you?" She struggled to her feet. "Dammit," she said when he had to move forward and help her.

He smiled. "When's the baby coming?"

"I'm pretty sure she's a giraffe, not a baby," she muttered, rubbing her belly. "Three weeks to go still, but you're not here looking for a trip down memory lane."

He'd worked here in high school and it'd been more home than anywhere he'd ever been. Here he'd been given food and shelter and comfort, and he'd have worked for free, but Quinn had insisted on paying him. "I don't know if I ever thanked you for the job," he started but Quinn shook her head.

"Don't thank me," she said on a fond smile. "You worked your ass off for us, and we were lucky to have you."

A little surprised by the emotion her words—and the memories—brought, he nodded. Quinn squeezed his hand and called out to her chef. "Breakfast special, extra bacon." She pointed to a chair. "Sit, you can eat and keep me company. When are you going to tell Tilly you're back?"

He grimaced. "She knows. I'm taking her class. She's not exactly thrilled."

Tilly laughed. "Let me guess. You figured it'd be hard to murder you in broad daylight."

He grimaced again and she shook her head, still smiling. "What you need to do is tell her the truth, Dylan. The whole truth." She met his gaze and sighed. "Which you're not going to do." She tossed up her hands. "Never did meet two more stubborn people."

Dylan smiled. "Then you should look in the mirror sometime."

An hour later, he was in the air, taking a local winery CEO and a few of his staff for a flyover of the entire area. They were interested in purchasing more land, but wanted to see it from a bird's view.

By the time he got back to the airport, the group was eager to book more flights as gifts to their customers for buying incentives. Dylan, Ric, and Penn had mapped out their upcoming month's flight schedule when his alarm beeped.

He rose. "Gotta go."

"I don't see a flight on the schedule," Penn said.

Ric was watching Dylan's face. "It's not a flight. It's Tilly."

"It's class," Dylan corrected.

"There's no class on Tuesdays," Ric said.

"I know, it's a field trip."

Penn grinned. "Is that what the kids are calling it these days?"

Dylan ignored them as he headed to the door.

"Dylan."

He turned back and Penn's smile was gone. "Took you long enough."

"To what?"

"To come back to the land of the living."

Ric nodded his agreement. "We're happy for you, man. We were getting worried about you."

Dylan scrubbed a hand down his face. They'd all been overseas together. They'd all seen and done stuff they didn't want to think about, much less even discuss. They'd all changed at their very core because of it.

But Dylan had been the only one of them to almost not make it back. "It's not what you think," he said. "Tilly's not into me like that anymore. She's still really angry."

"You could change that by telling her what happened to you," Ric said.

"No. The past is staying in the past," he said firmly.

"You sure about that?" Rick asked. "That's what you really want?"

Those were two very different questions.

Ric rose and came close, poking a finger into Dylan's chest. "Look man, you've led with your head for years and it saved all our asses on more than one occasion. It also kept you sane. But you're back now, we're all back, and we're safe. It's time to try a different tactic to life than just surviving."

Dylan looked at Penn, who nodded his agreement, and

then Dylan let out a rough laugh. "Are we, three hardened assholes, seriously having a discussion on our *feelings*?"

"Sounds like it," Ric said, still serious, still not playing. "But to be honest, there's only one of us here who's still burying his."

"Hey, just because I haven't been fucking my way through my contacts—"

"Because you haven't let anything go *deeper* than fucking around," Ric corrected.

"This is a ridiculous conversation and I'm done having it," Dylan said and headed out.

Tilly had sent a group email to class. The Town of Wildstone's tourist committee had put out a contest for the design of a local billboard meant to bring tourism traffic through town, and Tilly thought as a class they could win the design hands down. She wanted everyone to get a look at the actual billboard in person before they worked up their submission. Showing up today was entirely voluntary. His worry was that *no one* would show up and that it would hurt her feelings.

The billboard was located on a two lane windy highway road between the freeway and the ocean. He got there a few minutes early and was surprised to see students there. Getting out of his truck, he moved closer, counting heads. Literally everyone had come. He turned and found Tilly's eyes on his.

He smiled.

She didn't. But . . . she didn't look as irritated at the sight of him as she had the day before yesterday. *Prog-*

ress. He listened as she enthusiastically told everyone her plan for the billboard.

"As you know, town's looking for a design to attract tourists off the freeway and into downtown to bring attention to the local commerce. The art gallery is sponsoring the billboard," she said.

"Hey," one of her students said, eyes on his phone. "I just looked up the art gallery. You're having a show there in a few weeks," he said. "Cool."

"I am," Tilly said, cheeks flushed, looking happy.

It was a good look on her. He knew she wasn't making much. She'd done a few shows and sold some of her art. She also put in weekly shifts at the café she and Quinn still owned.

And now here she was, off the clock, doing this for the love of it, and watching her, Dylan saw what an amazing teacher she really was.

"Everyone take out the sketch pads I asked you to bring," she said. "Just off the cuff, show me what comes to mind for the billboard."

She walked around, taking in what the students were drawing, smiling and encouraging each. She saved Dylan for last, stopping at his side and silently looking down at his sketch pad.

"What's that?" she asked.

The only thing he could draw. "The schematic of the inside of the Bell's engine compartment."

Her eyes met his and there was a very slight hint of amusement in them. "Interesting design," she said.

He had to smile. "You're humoring me because I suck at drawing."

"Yes." She patted his hand and walked away. But . . . she'd touched him.

More progress.

Chapter 4

I said I was smart. I never said I had my shit together.

—from "The Mixed-Up Files of
Tilly Adams's Journal"

Ten years prior:

IN HINDSIGHT, TILLY would've said she wasn't good in an emergency of any sort. She tended to panic first, think later. And in a way, that's just what she did at Dylan's dad's house. She panicked. Didn't think. Just hit him over the head with her glass soda bottle.

He went down like a sack of rocks.

"Dylan," she said on a sob as her legs finally gave way. "Oh my God." Her vision wavered.

When she blinked the cobwebs clear, she was outside, Dylan tugging her down the street. A hundred yards from the house, he finally stopped.

Trembling all over, she sank to the wild grass. Dylan

did too, on his knees in front of her, still bleeding and looking pissed.

"I told you to stay away," he said grimly. "I told you I didn't need you or your help."

"But you did need me," she said and reached out to touch the cut over his eye.

He flinched away. "How did you get here?"

"Bus."

"Christ," he muttered and swiped his arm over his bleeding lip. "You're going to have to go back the same way, and do it now in case anyone calls the cops."

"Dylan—"

"Now, Tilly. Go now."

"Why?" She gasped and covered her mouth. "Omigod. Did I kill him?"

"No." He pulled her up to her feet and gave her a little push. "You were never here, got it?"

THAT NIGHT TILLY sat on Quinn and Mick's kitchen countertop eating ice cream out of the container with a wooden spoon.

Quinn was doing the same with a different carton at the table, but with her other hand she was also eating a pickle.

Tilly shuddered.

"About two weeks ago," Quinn said, "our TV remote went missing. Finally bought a new one, and guess what

I found in the freezer next to the ice cream just now? Our remote!"

Tilly shook her head. "I don't know what's more impressive, you losing your mind so thoroughly, or that it's been two weeks since you ate ice cream."

Quinn laughed and offered Leo—dozing in her lap—a lick of ice cream.

"Stop spoiling him," Tilly said.

Leo turned three circles in Quinn's shrinking lap and managed to make himself comfortable enough to close his eyes.

"Aw," Quinn said. "This is the best kind of kid to have. He doesn't talk back."

"Hey," her nine-year-old daughter, Natalie, said from where she was sitting on the counter next to Tilly.

Tilly laughed and hugged her adorable niece. "And what if I have a kid someday who's allergic to dogs and I have to get rid of the kid?" she asked.

Natalie giggled.

Mick was sitting across from Quinn, shaking his head in horror at what his wife was eating. "I thought the combination of pickle and ice cream gives you heartburn?"

"*Breathing* gives me heartburn," Quinn said.

"Yeah, Daddy," Natalie said. "And it gives her gas too."

Quinn pointed her pickle at her daughter. "That was our little secret."

Natalie giggled again. "Hard to keep things like farting a secret, Mom. Plus, it was in Target and you tried to make me take the blame for it."

Mick grinned and pulled Natalie in for a hug. "You know your mom's going to be mad at me now, right?"

"Because now you know she farts a lot?"

Mick burst out laughing. So did Tilly.

Quinn groaned and covered her face. "You're all going to be sorry someday when I'm gone and you have no one to laugh at."

Tilly's smile went from amused to nostalgic.

"What?" Quinn asked.

Tilly shrugged. "Mom used to say that."

"Help me up," Quinn demanded of Mick, who hoisted her out of the chair. She then moved to Tilly at the counter and wrapped her arms around her.

Tilly sighed. When Quinn was pregnant, she got very emotional. And very huggy. There was no fighting it so she hugged her sister back and set her head on her shoulder.

Natalie tapped on Tilly's shoulder and then crawled into her lap to join the hug. Tilly felt her throat tighten and her eyes burn. She had no idea where she would be without Quinn in her life. And by extension, Mick and Natalie. They were her family, her only family, and they meant everything. Quinn sniffled and Tilly knew she felt the same.

"Can we have pizza now?" Nat asked between them.

Tilly laughed, relieved the emotional moment was over, thwarted by the mention of pizza. "Yes, please."

After dinner, Quinn walked Tilly out. The night was gloriously clear, nothing but stars glittering like diamonds across a black velvet night.

"So what's up?" Quinn asked. "You're . . . off."

"I'm not."

"Liar."

Tilly sighed. "It's no big deal."

"Then spit it out."

"I'm suddenly feeling . . ." She tossed up her hands. "This weird sense of disappointment that I'm not some famous artist." She waited for Quinn to laugh.

But her sister slipped an arm around her waist and didn't laugh. "You're feeling dissatisfied with your life."

Tilly'd had goals for herself. She hadn't met them. Dylan'd had goals too, and though things hadn't happened as he'd planned, he'd done something with his life. Something pretty amazing. He'd served his country. He'd seen the world, flying as a pilot for hire. And now he was his own boss. He'd gone from punk-ass kid to soldier to pilot to businessman.

And she . . . well, she dabbled in the arts. "Yeah," she said to her sister. "I'm dissatisfied. There's an art fair in San Luis Obispo this weekend and I didn't get chosen to be in it. It feels worthless, Quinn. I'm a nobody. I've done nothing with myself."

"Stop it. You're a great teacher."

"I've been teaching for a week and a half," Tilly said dryly.

Quinn shook her head. "What's really wrong?"

Tilly sighed again. "Dylan's in town."

Quinn expressed no surprise and Tilly froze. "You knew," she breathed. "You knew and *you didn't tell me*?"

"I knew only because I'm a nosy-ass wife. Dylan contacted Mick a few weeks ago looking for an attorney to draw up a partnership agreement for Wildstone Air Tours. I read the email. Trust me, I wanted to tell you—"

"But you didn't."

"Only because I knew it should come from him, not me. I knew he'd want to tell you he was back himself."

Tilly laughed in disbelief. And hurt. And anger. "And what about what I would want? Or doesn't that matter?"

"Tilly—"

"No, Quinn. No. I'm your sister. You *know* what he did to me, you *know* how I felt after he deserted me."

Quinn bit her lower lip.

"*What?*"

"He never deserted you. He went away to give you the chance for a good life."

Tilly stared at her. "Are you *kidding* me? You know this how?" When Quinn opened her mouth, Tilly put up her hand to stop her from speaking. "No, never mind. Don't talk. I don't want to hear you talk right now."

"Tilly—"

She turned and got in her car. As she pulled out of the driveway, she caught sight of her sister standing on the sidewalk looking ten years pregnant, her arms wrapped around herself, and Tilly had to squash a flash of guilt to maintain her righteous anger.

She drove around for a bit, unsettled. Unhappy. Seeing Dylan, talking to him, had brought back a bunch of feelings from when she'd been a silly kid with silly hopes and dreams.

She'd been so naive.

Did he see her that way too?

She finally ended up at Mason's place. They didn't hang out as much as they used to but he was still a good friend. He lived in an apartment complex filled with mostly college students and shared a three bedroom with four other guys. He answered the door with a smile on his face, which faded quickly. "What's wrong?"

"Nothing," she said. "Everything."

"I've got a good way to solve your pain." He waggled a brow. "Naked, of course."

"We no longer soothe our collective pain," she said. "We agreed about a year ago to stop doing that."

"You agreed," Mason said. "I'm just respecting your wishes."

It was true. She hadn't been with anyone in a long time. But though Mason was very attractive, she wasn't feeling men right now.

Liar, a little voice inside her whispered. You're feeling *Dylan.*

"The bar," Mason said, reading her expression, taking her rejection good-naturedly, which was one reason he was such a good friend. "We're going to the bar."

"I'm broke."

"My treat," he said.

"You're broke too."

"There's always money for a beer." He put her into his car and off they went.

The Whiskey River Bar and Grill was the only game in town for nightlife. Which meant it was packed. Tilly was surprised to see that they'd even cleared some tables and put up a makeshift dance floor, which was rocking tonight.

"It's the owner's birthday," Mason said. "Boomer wanted a dance party. Want to dance?"

Tilly heard him, but her gaze was caught and held by someone at the other end of the bar.

Dylan.

He was with Ric and Penn, but he broke away from them and came toward her until they stood toe to toe. "Sorry," she said to Mason. "I can't dance. I have to yell at someone."

Mason divided a look between them, lifted his hands, and backed away, but not before muttering "good luck" to Dylan beneath his breath.

Dylan didn't take his dark, serious eyes off Tilly.

"You talked to my sister," she said. "You didn't talk to me, but you talked to Quinn." Having heard enough, she turned to leave, but Boomer took the mic.

"Everyone on the dance floor," he said. "I want to dance with my wife and have you all with us."

Tilly turned to leave but Dylan reached out and snagged her hand, moving slow enough that she could have easily evaded him if she wanted to. But apparently she didn't want that because she let him wrap his warm fingers in hers and lead her to the dance floor, when he pulled her into his leanly muscled body. She opened her mouth to say something, not really even sure what that might be, but he put a finger to her lips.

"I can't go back and change things," he said. "And to be honest, I'm not sure I would. I didn't have a single say about my life back then, no control, no power, nothing, Tee. I was helpless, and . . ." He shook his head and pulled her in even closer so that she could no longer see his face. "I hated that most of all. Hated too that you saw me that way."

She flashed back to those long-ago nights when he'd crawl in her bedroom window bloody and bruised, and felt her heart clutch hard. "I wanted to kill him for you," she said fiercely. "I wanted to kill him with my bare hands."

A long exhale escaped him and he pulled her in closer. "I didn't think I was capable of love back then, and I wasn't. Not until you. I loved you, God I loved you, but I had nothing to offer you."

"Don't you get it?" she asked, tilting her head up to his. "I didn't need you to offer me anything but you."

"Tee." His voice was low, husky, and he kissed her. It started out sweet and gentle but didn't stay that way for long. By the time they broke free, they'd generated enough heat to raise the temperature of the entire room. Time seemed to stand still as they stared into each other's eyes. Tilly didn't breathe, and was pretty sure he didn't either.

Then the song ended and the music changed to a fast song, and still they stood there, eyes locked. Finally, Dylan shook his head slightly as if to clear it and reached for her.

"I've gotta go," she whispered, and pulling free, walked out into the cool night and gulped in some desperately needed air.

Chapter 5

> How long are you supposed to go between gym
> visits? Six months? A year? Just trying to get it
> right the first time I go.
>
> —from "The Mixed-Up Files of
> Tilly Adams's Journal"

Ten years prior:

IT'D BEEN DAYS since Tilly had gone to Dylan's dad's house and she hadn't heard from him until he finally sent her a text to meet him at the park.

Tilly climbed out her window and found him, a lone dark shadow sitting on a swing, his foot down and anchoring him to the sand beneath.

Feeling shaky with relief, Tilly sat next to him. She wanted to soak him up, but instead mirrored his position, head tipped back, staring at the stars.

"Tilly . . ." He blew out a sigh and she heard him shift

and felt the weight of his gaze. She didn't look. She was very busy counting the stars.

"Tilly," he said again, voice low. Tense. Anguished. "I'm sorry."

Her heart squeezed. Dammit.

"I hate that you saw me like that," he said roughly. "I hate . . ." He paused and when he spoke, the words sounded like he had to drag them over shards of glass. "I hate that you know what my life's like."

Now her heart seemed swollen, unable to fit in her rib cage, and she turned to him, reaching out for his hand.

He hesitated and then took it in his bigger, callused one.

"And I hate it for you," she whispered.

They sat like that for a long time, just watching the sky.

DYLAN WOKE UP before the crack of dawn the next morning. Actually, that was inaccurate. You couldn't wake up if you hadn't slept. Instead, he'd spent a good amount of the dark hours reliving the kiss he'd laid on Tilly. He'd actually forgotten how explosive their chemistry was.

Good to know that some things never changed.

But the darker the night got, the darker his thoughts got as well. Their chemistry hadn't changed, but *he* had. Maybe too much.

Giving up on sleep, he got out of bed. Growing up, he'd gotten pretty good at functioning on low to no sleep, a skill he'd further honed in the military. It'd been a way of life for a long time.

Funny how fast a guy could get accustomed to relative safety and not having to spend every living waking moment worried about watching your own six.

He showered to clear his head and left, knowing he was way too early for his first flight. But he had a pit stop to make. And thanks to an angry spring storm, he was going to do it in the pouring rain.

He parked in the cemetery lot, noting that he was the only one there as he wound his way in the pouring rain through the graveyard.

As he'd never been here before, it took him forty-five minutes to find the right grave, and by the time he did, water ran off him in rivulets. He squatted in front of the gravestone and paused. "Sorry, I haven't been." He shook his head. "No, scratch that. That was a lie. I'm not sorry. I intended to *never* come, but apparently you're still haunting me." He took in a deep breath, let it out. "You were an asshole, Dad. But you're dead and you can't shape my life anymore. And you know what else? I forgive you, you sorry sack of shit. I forgive you."

And with that, he rose to his full height and walked away, not feeling any lighter for it.

He skipped class and walked into the airport, his wet shoes squeaking with every step, and both Penn and Ric stood up from behind the front desk and began clapping.

Dylan stared at them. "Are you guys still drunk?"

"No," Ric said. "We're clapping because that was some kiss you laid on Tilly last night. Do you kiss all of our business associates that way? Because I've gotta admit, I'm feeling left out."

Dylan flipped him off and headed to the Bell 206. Of course the idiots followed.

"You guys getting back together?" Penn asked.

Dylan thought of how Tilly had walked away last night. "No."

"Why not?"

"No questions before caffeine," Dylan said.

Penn went to the corner where they had a coffeepot for clients, poured a cup, and brought it to Dylan. "You still haven't told her why you left town?"

"No, he didn't."

They all whipped around at the sound of Tilly's voice. Penn had the good grace to look slightly embarrassed. Ric merely poured another cup of coffee. This one he added milk and sugar to, and brought over to Tilly.

She gave him a long look, rolled her eyes, and then took it and sipped. "Thank you." Then she looked at Dylan. "Don't let me stop you. Please, continue your conversation."

"We were done," Dylan said.

"Were you? Because it seems to me like maybe you were about to answer a question that Penn asked you."

"I don't think so," Penn said, trying to look innocent, Dylan's best friend to the end.

But Tilly wasn't buying the bullshit Penn was selling. She didn't take her eyes off Dylan. She wanted answers, that much was clear.

But before he could say anything, Leo broke loose from Tilly and scrambled for purchase on the smooth concrete floor. For a moment he looked like a cat on linoleum, but he got his footing and headed straight for Dylan, barking his fool little head off the whole time.

"Arf, arf, ARF!"

Dylan held his ground, thinking how much damage could a six-pound rat do anyway? When Leo got to Dylan's feet, he stopped short, snarling and growling menacingly.

"Leo, stop!" Tilly said.

Leo did not stop. "Arf, arf, ARF!"

Dylan decided enough was enough. He squatted down to get eye to eye with the dog. "Only one of us can be the alpha," he said.

Leo stopped barking for a moment to take this in and the silence was heavenly but short lived as he started in again.

"Arf, arf, ARF!"

Shaking his head, Dylan rose to his feet. Lost cause and he knew when to cut his losses, on both the girl *and* her dog. He turned to walk away and felt Leo clamp his teeth onto his pants leg. "You serious?" he asked.

Leo growled, not letting loose.

"Things to do, little man," he said and headed toward

Tilly, towing Leo along with him as he went. "I've got something of yours."

"I'm sorry. Leo!" She bent to scoop the puppy up and he immediately stopped barking and panted happily at Tilly, licking her chin. She kept her eyes on Dylan. "You were about to explain some things to me."

"Is that why you're here?" he asked, hoping to divert.

"No. I'm here because . . ." She avoided looking at Penn and Ric. "Because you missed class."

"You wanted me to drop your class."

"Yes, but not because . . ." She hesitated. "Of a kiss."

"I had a flight I couldn't miss," he said. "Would the teacher like a note?"

"Nope," she said. "I'd like that explanation."

Dylan sent a long "leave" look to Penn and Ric, both of whom were standing there like two middle school boys hoping for gossip. Neither of whom left. Dylan cleared his throat and jerked his head toward the door.

"The short version of the story," Penn said to Tilly instead of leaving, "is that he acted like a dick, but he did it for you."

Ric wrapped an arm around Penn's neck and slapped a hand over the guy's mouth. "Ignore us," he said to Dylan. "Pretend we're not even here."

"And the long version?" Tilly asked Penn.

Penn tore Ric's hand from his mouth. "He went into the military so you'd take your art scholarship. He did it so you'd move on and not look back. He did it so you'd have the life you dreamed of having. And he tried to not look back too. But then when he nearly got blown up and landed in the hospital at death's door—"

Tilly gasped.

"No, it's okay," Penn assured her. "It was four years ago now. He lived."

Tilly turned on Dylan. "You were hurt? And you didn't tell me?"

Dylan opened his mouth, but Penn beat him to it. "He forced himself not to keep up with you, so we all looked you up on Facebook to see what you were up to. And you were seeing someone, so he refused to let us get in touch with you—"

"Wait." Her mouth fell open. "You decided from a Facebook post to not to contact me?"

"Never said our boy wasn't stubborn," Penn said. His smile faded. "But it was really bad, Tilly. He wasn't in a good place to make decisions, you know? In the end, we respected his wishes and bullied him back to the land of the living with the carrot of starting our own business flying for hire."

"Okay," Dylan said tightly. "*Out.*"

Tilly turned to go, but he snagged her hand. "Not you."

"Right," Ric said and picked up Leo before dragging Penn toward the offices. "We'll dog sit."

Penn twisted back to Tilly. "If you've got any other questions, just ask him. If after hearing his story you're not punched in the feels and inclined to forgive him, you might want to check your pulse."

TILLY WAITED UNTIL Penn and Ric were out of sight and it was just her and Dylan. She had so many emotions swirling through her, she could hardly breathe, and questions too. So many questions, but he was drenched. "Aren't you cold?" she asked. "Do you need to change?"

He took her by the hand and tugged her along with him down the hall to an office. He shut the door and went straight to the duffel bag on the desk, pulling out a change of clothes. She expected him to excuse himself to another room. She did not expect him to begin stripping out of his clothes.

He kicked off his athletic shoes first, then his socks, which hit the floor with a soggy "smack." He pulled off his windbreaker, which had been suctioned to his chest and back and made a very wet pop as he freed himself of it, like the nylon didn't want to let go of him.

She kinda knew how it felt.

Before she could get annoyed at herself for the thought, he pulled his T-shirt over his head and then his hands went to his jeans.

"What do you think you're doing?" For the record, she hadn't looked away, but let her eyes soak up his bare chest and abs.

One hundred percent, the too skinny teenager had filled out in all the right places.

He glanced up. "I'm changing out of my wet clothes into dry ones."

"Here?"

Instead of answering, he turned to rifle through the

duffel bag and then shoved his jeans and boxers down and off, leaving him buck-ass naked.

With a shocked squeak, she covered her eyes, but when she heard his soft chuckle, she peeked out between her fingers.

"You've seen it all before," he reminded her, pulling on a pair of black knit boxers before shaking out a pair of jeans.

"A long time ago!"

He looked amused as he pulled up the jeans and adjusted himself. "Nothing much has changed that I know of."

That wasn't true. He'd gone from boy to man, and his body reflected that. Utterly unable to stop herself, she moved toward him and ran a hand over the sleek, smooth muscles of his back as they shifted with his movements.

At her touch, he froze. Still turned away from her, he tipped his head back, eyes closed, and said her name in a low, husky, desire-filled whisper.

Swallowing hard, she watched her fingers trace a line down his spine, stopping only when the waistband of his jeans blocked her path. He'd left to give her a life, misguided and stupid as that was, not because he'd stopped feeling for her. He'd been hurt, badly . . . almost died.

"Keep doing that," he murmured, still not moving, "and we're going to break in my office with your bare ass on my desk and me buried deep inside you."

She let her hand slip into the back of his jeans, loose since he hadn't buttoned them.

"Tilly," he said, his voice soft but the warning was

clear. "Use your words. Tell me what you want or stop touching me."

She knew what she didn't want. She didn't want to be warned away. She was tired of thinking. Tired of feeling ... empty. She wanted to feel something, and the last person to make her really do that was Dylan. It felt right, and so did the handful of taut ass she squeezed.

He turned toward her, his eyes dark with desire as he caught her hands in his and drew them up and around his neck. "Say it, Tilly. I need to hear you say it."

"I want you."

He pressed his forehead to hers and closed his eyes. "Again."

"I want you, Dylan. I always have."

He sucked in a breath and his arms tightened on her. "Now?"

"Yes."

"Here?"

"*Yes.*"

He lifted her up against him and set her onto his desk. Holding her gaze, he leaned past her and swept the desk clear, letting everything hit the floor.

It gave her both a laugh and a ridiculous shiver.

But Dylan wasn't playing. "Cold?" he asked, his hands gliding up the outside of her thighs, encouraging them open so he could step in between, snugging their bodies up against each other.

"No. It was the cheesy gesture of knocking everything off your desk that got me."

He met her gaze and at whatever he saw in hers, smiled. "I've got more cheesy moves."

"Bring 'em on."

He gave her one last very hot, very amused look before his mouth came down on hers. This kiss, unlike his others, was serious and most definitely heading somewhere, and it thrilled her. She explored his chest with her hands, slowly relearning the feel of him, following that with her mouth because she needed a taste.

With a groan, his hands went to her hips, squeezed, and then slid beneath the hem of her dress, his fingers toying with the lace edging on her undies.

"Dylan," she whispered as his fingers found his way beneath the lace to tease her bare flesh, making her moan his name and him groan at finding her so ready for him.

One tug and she was bared to him, and it only took her a second to push his jeans back down and free him.

Their gazes met again and she could see the need and hunger she felt mirrored back at her.

But also a hint of doubt.

"Tilly—" he started but she surged up and took his mouth with hers.

"I want this," she reminded him. "I want tonight, whatever we can give each other."

Producing a condom, he leaned down and gave a soft, loving kiss that so thoroughly disarmed her that she gasped when he slid home. She was instantly swept away, lost in the sensations as he enveloped her into his arms and took her with a slow, steady rhythm that grew an ache into a flame, and a flame into a flash fire that consumed her.

Somehow she managed to open her eyes and watch the intensity on his face, which moved her almost beyond bearing. "Dylan," she whispered.

He inhaled sharply and let out an unsteady breath, leaning into her to bury his face in the crook of her neck. His heat seeped through her so that she no longer felt the chill of the desk beneath her bare ass.

"You feel so damn good," he murmured, nuzzling and kissing her neck, her jaw, her ear, all while continuing to move inside her until she let go with a cry of pleasure that took him along with her.

Her senses took a moment to return, a long moment, and the first thing she heard was a tinny male voice from somewhere on the floor.

"Hey, man, either you're calling for help or butt dialing me." Penn. "But it sounds like a good time is being had in there. *Hello*? Open the office door and let Leo in, he's sitting there wanting his mama."

Dylan picked up the fallen phone and hit Disconnect.

Tilly opened the door and let Leo in before biting her lower lip, torn between horror and laughter. "Oh my God. They heard—"

"I'm sorry," Dylan said, "but I promise you, they won't ever say anything to you about it. Not if they want to live."

Laughter won.

Dylan looked at her with wry amusement. "Still think I'm smooth?"

Chapter 6

Sometimes my great accomplishment is just keeping my mouth shut.

—from "The Mixed-Up Files of Tilly Adams's Journal"

Ten years prior:

TILLY WATCHED OUT the window until she saw Dylan show up for work. She'd texted him to come a little early, but he hadn't. She'd had to be quick to catch him getting out of his car before he entered the café.

"Thought you'd come over and see me," she said.

"Can't. I've got work. And you have to study for finals this week."

"I'm taking a day off from studying," she said.

"No, you're not."

She stared at his back as he turned away, hurt to the core that he didn't want to be with her. "What do you care?"

He turned to face her again, eyes dark, expression dark. Hell, his life was dark. "You think I don't care?"

She swallowed as he strode back to her and glared down into her eyes. "I spend more time on your school-work than mine," he said. "I check on you every single night that I can get away. I'm working more hours than I have in a day so that after I give most of my pay to my mom to cover her rent, I can put a little bit away for a future that I'm not even sure exists."

Tilly felt her throat burn. "It does."

His face softened. "I'm going to go to work, Tee. And you're going to study. We need the money and the edu-cation."

She held her breath. "We?"

"Yeah." And then he did something he rarely did—he touched her. He cupped her face in his big, callused hands and dropped his forehead to hers. "It's all about the we," he murmured. "Don't ever think otherwise."

TILLY REDRESSED HERSELF and watched Dylan do the same, not wanting to miss a thing. The image of his very fine bod was now permanently burned into her brain, where it would most certainly fuel her fantasies for many nights to come. But then she froze.

Because his knees. Both were marked up with mul-tiple harsh-looking scars that looked terrifyingly real. "Ouch," she said softly.

He shrugged and once again stepped into a pair

of jeans, pulling them up. "Guess some things have changed," he admitted. "And yeah, it was a bitch." He dug past some things in the bag and came up with a T-shirt.

"You don't even limp," she marveled.

He shrugged on the shirt. "Rehab was brutal," he admitted. "Thought I was tough going in, but I wasn't. Not even close."

"How did you get through?"

He turned to face her. "Penn and Ric. They pretty much bullied me into it."

She nodded like she was all calm, but she wasn't. Wasn't feeling anywhere near calm. "So," she said, trying to sound reasonable when she felt anything but. "You bailed on me, having made the decision for me that I deserved more than you could give me. You gave up your dreams and went into the military, all to get away from me."

"I didn't give up on anything," he said. "The military was a way to keep my astronaut dream alive."

Okay, she could understand that. "Until you got hurt," she guessed.

He gave a brief nod of agreement. "I'd qualified and gone through flight school."

"And then . . . you were hurt," she guessed. "What happened?"

"On a recon mission, we were given bad intel." He shrugged. "We took on fire as we were heading back to base."

"How bad?" she whispered.

"Not as bad as Penn made it sound. I took a spray of bullets across my knees. Not life threatening."

"Penn said—"

"—I nearly bled out before help arrived. Would have, if Ric hadn't been there to yell at me that if I died, he'd follow me to hell, and that then his mother would come haunt the both of us for all of eternity."

"Him yelling at you kept you alive?"

He gave her a small smile. "That, and the fact that he literally hooked us up to each other with fuel tubing he ripped out of the tank and used to give me his blood. Good thing we shared a blood type, huh?"

Dear God. Picturing the circumstances, the utter chaos they'd been in, and the unbelievably heroic actions of the people who served overseas had her throat tightening. "He's a good friend."

"Yeah. They both are."

And they'd been there for him when she hadn't. Couldn't. Because he'd shut her out. "You were discharged."

"Had both knees replaced, which meant no getting into the astronaut program and in fact, no more flying for me. Not for the military and not as an astronaut."

She looked down at his leg, covered in his pants. "You've had a remarkable recovery."

"Long-ass road through PT." He lifted a shoulder. "I was . . . determined. Because I wasn't going to give up flying. I could go private."

She nodded, her chest feeling too tight for her rib cage. He'd never given up. Not like she had . . . "Why didn't you come home?"

He met her gaze. "Wildstone wasn't really home for me."

She felt the air back up in her lungs at that.

"The only place that had ever felt like home to me was being wherever you were," he said quietly and took a step closer.

Leo picked his head up off Tilly's shoulder and growled.

"Zip it, Leo," she said, staring up at Dylan. "Except you looked me up, determined I was off the market by one photo, and didn't bother."

"Are you saying you weren't?" he asked. "Off the market?"

She looked away. Because the truth was, none of the men in her past had ever made her feel what Dylan had. "I'm saying it doesn't matter. You wanted me to forget about you."

"I did," he said, and ignoring Leo's low growl, reached out, running a finger along her temple, tucking a stray strand of hair behind her ear. "But I never forgot about you."

She shook her head. "Why are you here now then? You guys could have started up your company anywhere."

"Ric got a deal here at this airport. And I told myself that eight years is a long time. A lifetime. That you'd moved on and so had I."

She stared up at him. "So now what?"

He gave a slow shake of his head. "Yesterday, I'd have said we just ignore our past and deal with the here and now. Live our lives the way we've been living them. Separately."

"And now?" she asked, inexplicably holding her breath on his answer.

"And now, the ball's in your court." He gave Leo a very hard look. "I'm going to move in close," he warned the dog. "Don't even think about using your teeth on me." And with that, he leaned in and kissed Tilly.

Like yesterday's kiss, it was gentle. Sweet.

And no less devastatingly sexy for it. She heard a soft, surprised moan. Her own. She couldn't help it—at the touch of his tongue to hers, memories exploded, playing across her eyelids. This man had been her first, and God help her but she wanted him to be her last . . . With that thought she broke free and stared up at him. "I thought you just said the ball's in my court?"

"It is. I just believe in stacking the deck."

Chapter 7

After experiencing "feelings," I've decided they're not for me, but thanks for the opportunity.

**—from "The Mixed-Up Files of
Tilly Adams's Journal"**

Ten years prior:

TILLY'S HEART DID a little happy dance as she tiptoed out of the quiet house and made it to the park in a record-breaking three minutes.

The place was deserted. No one on the swings. So she walked past the swing set to their tree, and the tree house. In the dark, she could see the glow of a phone screen. She climbed up and found a tall, lanky figure sitting there and her pulse sped up even as her smile faded.

Dylan was hiding from the world and that meant he was hurting.

She plopped down next to him. "Hey."

Dylan lay flat on his back and stared up at the stars. "Wouldn't mind being an astronaut."

Her heart caught. He had the grades for it. Or he would've had the grades for it if he hadn't had to work his ass off on top of school. "You could totally do it," she said, lying down next to him so that their arms brushed. She touched his fingers with hers. "You could do whatever you want."

He snorted and she wondered what had happened to upset him. She'd ask, but he wouldn't tell her so she did her best to look him over to see if he had new injuries. Thankfully, she didn't see any. "You can," she whispered. "Be an astronaut."

"Says who?"

"My mom." Her breath caught because it was a reminder that she was gone now. "She always told me that."

Dylan rolled to his side and propped his head up with his hand as he studied her in the dark. "She was trying to be nice. Nobody gets to do what they want. When school's out, I'm going to have to dig trenches for my dad."

He already worked as many hours a week as he could spare to help his mom cover expenses. "Once you graduate, you can do whatever you want."

"Don't be naive, Tee."

She pulled her fingers from his and sat up. She hated when he acted like he was so much older than she was. Hated when he made her feel like a stupid little kid. "I'm not naive." She pulled her knees in and pressed her forehead to them. "But sometimes, you just have to believe in *something*."

He blew out a sigh and sat up beside her. She felt his hand brush over her hair and wrap around her and he pulled her in closer. "I'm sorry. I'm an asshole."

"You're not." She turned her face to look up at him. "You aren't like your dad, Dylan."

His expression hardened at the thought. "And I'm never going to be."

"Good." She hesitated because he didn't like to be told what to do. Hated it actually, because so many of his choices had been taken from him. And she didn't want to make things worse, but she really wanted to say something. "And just as you don't have to be the dick your dad is," she said carefully, "you also don't have to follow his chosen profession. You do whatever the hell you want to do. And you've got me at your back. You know I've been helping out at the café in the mornings and Quinn insists on paying me. I'm going to save every penny in case you need it. Do you hear me?"

A ghost of a smile twitched at his mouth. "I hear you. So do the people in China. But I'm not going to take your money, ever. I'm saving mine too, I'll be okay."

"So why would you go be a laborer when summer hits? Why wouldn't you do something you love? Like work at the rec center and help coach the little kids in baseball?" He'd been a baseball superstar until he'd had to quit the team for his job. "Or you could be a lifeguard.

Lots of kids are doing that this summer and they're hiring."

"The class to become a certified lifeguard is three hundred bucks," he said. "The rec center won't hire me because I had to have a recommendation from my coach and the principal, and though the coach said I would be great in the job, the principal said I had a bad attitude and a temper."

This pissed her off. "That's not fair."

"I trashed his office when he accused me of stealing money from the cafeteria," he reminded her.

"Wrongly accused."

Dylan lifted a shoulder. Didn't matter. The damage was done. And now he would be digging ditches for his macho, sadistic father all summer and she'd be worried for him every single second of every single day.

HALFWAY THROUGH TILLY'S next day of class, she had the students working quietly on their billboard design while she walked around the classroom, tentatively impressed at what she was seeing.

They'd voted on a theme for their submission and had come up with just about the opposite of what Tilly could have imagined.

Love.

Her idea had been to divide the billboard space into a grid. Everyone would take their block and do what they wanted, but then have it fit together with the others like a puzzle, making one whole cohesive piece.

She glanced up at a movement from the classroom door and found Quinn standing there, waving at her.

Tilly drew a deep breath. They hadn't spoken in three days. Extremely unusual for them. Quinn had been butting into Tilly's life since she'd first stepped into it all those years ago.

With a sigh, Tilly moved to the door. "What?"

"Brought you cookies." Quinn handed her a tin. "Fresh baked. Double fudge. Soft and gooey."

"Baked with guilt?"

Quinn sighed. "You're still mad."

"I'm still mad," Tilly confirmed. She looked back at the class, relieved to find no one paying them any attention. Her voice lowered, she said, "I can't believe you didn't tell me about Dylan, about why he left, why he stayed gone, what happened to him . . . None of it."

Quinn's eyes were solemn and apologetic. "I only knew for a few weeks, and only because I'm nosy as hell. I wanted to tell you, but Mick thought that Dylan would want to tell you everything himself, so I promised Mick—"

"You made a promise to me too—to be my sister—"

"I *am* your sister," Quinn said. "If I'd told you back then, you'd have dropped out of school and run halfway across the world to be with him and he would've seen that as pity and shoved you away. I didn't want you hurt, Tilly. You both needed to grow up, and now you have—" Quinn broke off, her eyes widening slightly as she caught sight of something in the classroom. *Some-*

one. She grinned. "He's still in your class," she whispered. "Dylan."

Like there was any possibility of mistaking who she was talking about. Tilly glanced at Dylan, had a flashback to the other day in his office when he'd been buried deep inside her, and then got uncomfortably warm. She grabbed Quinn's hand. "Excuse me a sec, class, I'll be right back!" And then she tugged Quinn out into the hall and shut the classroom door.

"You didn't kick him out," Quinn said.

Ignoring her sister's smug and annoying grin, she counted to five for patience. None came. "Look," she said, reaching out to rub Quinn's huge belly. "You're ready to pop. What the hell are you doing here?"

"That's not the right question," Quinn said.

"I'm pretty sure it is."

"Nope." Quinn lifted her phone and snapped a pic of Tilly. "The right question is, why are you all flushed and bright-eyed?" She showed Tilly the pic of herself.

Dammit. She was indeed flushed and bright-eyed. "Maybe I'm enjoying teaching." She paused. "A lot," she admitted.

Quinn gasped, a hand to her heart as joy filled her expression. "Yeah?"

"Yeah." Tilly narrowed her eyes. "Wait—what are you doing?"

"Nothing," Quinn sniffed.

"You're crying. There's no crying in here! There's no crying in school!"

"I know." Quinn lifted the hem of her shirt and swiped at her eyes.

Tilly sighed.

"Well, sue me, I'm pregnant, okay? I cry at the drop of a hat! Or at the sight of my beautiful baby sister looking happy for once."

Tilly searched her pockets for tissues and came up with a napkin.

Quinn blew her nose noisily. "And it's not just the teaching making you look like that either."

"Stop trying to make my life a romance novel," Tilly said. "Romance does not make the world go round."

"No, but it makes it a better place. Tell me the truth. You still care about him."

Tilly opened her mouth but Quinn held up a finger. "Look me in the eyes when you attempt to deny it because you've never been able to look me in the eyes and lie."

Tilly looked her in the eyes. "*Dammit.*"

Quinn smiled. "I thought you were over him?"

"Shut up," Tilly said without heat. "Now go be pregnant."

Quinn laughed. "You're *not* over him. You like him."

Yeah. Yeah, she did, and she peered in the narrow window on her classroom door to catch sight of him. His head was bent in concentration with a handful of the students around him working in tandem on their projects.

It was terrifying how easily he fit back into her life and at the thought, her breath quickened. "I'm going to hyperventilate."

Quinn popped open the tin and shoved a cookie at her. "Here, eat this. It's impossible to eat one of my perfect cookies and hyperventilate."

Tilly shoved half a cookie into her mouth.

"See?"

Tilly shook her head. "I'm too broken for this," she said around a mouthful.

Quinn's smile faded and she hugged Tilly tight, nearly suffocating her. "Last I checked," she whispered against Tilly's jaw, "we're all a little broken." She pulled back to look into Tilly's eyes. "And yet we still live and breathe. And love."

THE SUN WAS just thinking of setting when Tilly watched Dylan pilot the helicopter in for a landing. She sipped from a specialty mug of tea that Ric had made for her and watched through the wall of windows of the hangar as Dylan helped his clients from the chopper, who surprised her by being two kids and their families.

"They're Make-A-Wish kids," Penn said, coming up beside her, looking out the window. "Dylan made it happen."

She watched as he ruffled one of the kids' hair. The kid lifted his arms and Dylan obliged, picking him up, swinging him up onto his shoulders as they walked around the helicopter. Dylan pointed out some things and then the next kid got the exact same treatment.

"He's showing them his post-flight check," Penn said.

"He's got this thing, especially after his injury and losing his dream." Penn met her gaze in the reflection of the window. "He likes to show kids you can come back from that and still fly, or whatever the hell it is you dream of."

The clients came in and Penn moved to greet them, effortlessly working his charismatic, charming host gig while Tilly watched Dylan conduct another post-flight check.

By the time he came in, hair tousled and cheeks reddened from the wind chill, dark aviator sunglasses covering his eyes, leather jacket stretched taut over broad shoulders, she'd forgotten what she'd come to say to him. All she wanted to do was get his mouth back on hers.

At the sight of her standing there, he pushed his sunglasses to the top of his head, his gaze surprised. "Hey."

"Hey."

He eyed her mug of tea and his gaze flicked to the hallway of the offices, where Ric stood. "For such a hardened war hero, you're an old lady, you know that?"

Ric just toasted him with his own mug of tea. "Takes one to know one, man." And then he was gone.

Dylan turned the full force of his attention on Tilly. "It's nice to see you," he said. "But what are you doing here?"

She pulled her lower lip in between her teeth and contemplated him. "Truth?"

"Always."

She drew a deep breath. "I came to discuss . . . what happened between us."

"Okay." His brown eyes were warm and curious. He was willing to listen to her.

Which was more than she could say for herself. At the thought, and against her own better sense, she felt herself soften. "I have questions," she said.

"Ask," he said easily. "I'll answer anything you've got."

She set down her tea and took a deep breath. "Why didn't you just tell me you were leaving and why. You knew I'd understand."

He hesitated.

"You said anything," she reminded him.

"I'm trying, but the truth is—and was—that you couldn't possibly have understood. *I* didn't, not even when it was happening to me."

She crossed her arms. "You didn't even try me," she said tightly.

He blew out a breath. "I wanted to make something of myself, and the sole reason I wanted that was because of you. You made me believe in myself enough to go for the astronaut dream. I didn't get there though."

He'd once been the most important person in her life, so it shouldn't shock her that she'd been his.

"But you tried. And you made it work for you regardless."

He shrugged.

"Dylan . . ." She spread her arms wide. "Look at me. I'm not exactly the world-famous artist I thought I'd be."

"You've still got your art," he said. "And your show in a week now."

She sucked in a breath of nerves at the reminder. "Yeah."

"I'm proud of you," he said. "And now you're spreading the joy of the art by teaching. You're doing good things, Tilly. I think you'd be happy if you let yourself be."

"And how about you?" she asked. "Are you letting yourself be happy?"

"I didn't. Not for a long time." He shook his head. "When I first got injured, I was angry. Really angry. And a part of me thought I'd probably turn into my father."

"You're never going to be like him," she said adamantly.

"How do you know?"

"I *know*."

He arched a disbelieving brow.

"I just saw you with those kids. They needed this, needed you, and you were amazing with them. If you really have any deep-seated fears of being like your father, take a good look at yourself today."

He lost a little bit of his remoteness with that and he held out his hand.

She stared at it. "What?"

"Trust me?"

"Yes," she said without hesitation.

He wiggled his fingers and she slipped her hand in his. He then led her out onto the tarmac and toward the Bell, pulling out his phone, calling Ric or Penn to let them know he was going back up with a plus one. Then he got her seated in the co-pilot seat and turned to her, checking her seat belt and handling his own. Then he slid the aviators down back over his eyes. "Ready?" he asked.

"For what?"

He smiled.

When they were in the air, her stomach was in her chest squishing her heart and she sat with her nose pressed up against the window, breathless with wonder.

"You okay?"

She nodded but didn't take her eyes off the sights. From up here she could see green rolling hills, dotted with lines of grape crops and oaks, outlined on one side by the shiny blue Pacific, white-capped and shimmering brilliantly. "The view, it's . . . beautiful."

"Mine's not bad either."

She met his gaze and rolled her eyes.

"Too cheesy?" he asked.

"Yes." But she'd liked it . . .

He pointed out to her left. "That's Wildstone. Wait for it . . ." A few seconds later, he nodded. "Caro's Café."

She saw her mom's café, and seeing it from an aerial view like this, for some reason her throat became tight. "Wow."

"You and Quinn kept it," he said. "And her house."

"We did." She kept her eyes to the window. "We thought about selling them a bunch of times, but it's all we have of her and we like feeling her there."

"Nothing wrong with holding on to good memories," he said quietly. "I've held on to mine."

She looked over at him then and they stared at each

other for a beat. "Did you ever get into any serious relationships?" she asked quietly. "After me?"

He shook his head. "I saw women here and there, but nothing serious. You?"

She let out a low laugh. "There's like ten different levels of dating now before you actually date. It's so confusing to me that it makes me need a nap."

Thirty minutes later, he brought them in for a smooth landing and turned to her. "Let me unconfused things for you."

"What?"

Leaning in, he pulled off her headset and let his fingers tighten in her hair. "We're actually dating. No nap required. Unless you want one, and I'll be happy to join you."

Chapter 8

I'm not like other girls, I know what I want for
dinner. I've been thinking about it since lunch.

—from "The Mixed-Up Files of
Tilly Adams's Journal"

Ten years prior:

"DID YOU STUDY?" Dylan asked.

In spite of wanting to cry, Tilly smiled at him because he cared about her so much it hurt. "Yes."

"Good." He stood and pulled her up. "You've got to go home before you get in trouble."

She stood close to him, very close—the toes of their battered sneakers touched. But since he was so much taller than she was, that was about all that lined up and she *ached*, ached, to be as tall because then she could feel him, thigh to thigh, chest to chest. Her breathing hitched just thinking about it.

Kiss me, she wished with all her might. *Please for once, kiss me . . .*

And maybe it was her turn for a miracle because he did. He bent and kissed the top of her head.

"Dylan," she whispered with all the longing in her heart, which felt like it might burst.

He stilled. "Tee—"

"Please?" she whispered, tipping back her head.

He groaned and crushed her to him. For the most perfect moment in all the moments of her entire life, he lowered his mouth to hers. Soft. Gentle. Patient.

But Tilly wasn't feeling any of those things, so she tugged him in even closer. Then, on a mission, she touched her tongue to his and . . . the kiss exploded.

It was like nothing she'd ever felt in her entire life as he hauled her in tight and kissed her deep. Her heart pounded, her skin felt too tight for her body, and she loved it.

But then he pulled away.

With a little mewl of protest, she tried to wrap herself around him, but he gripped her arms and held her off. "Tee. Tee, stop. We're not doing this."

"Why?" she demanded, and if he said it was because she was too young for him, she was going to—

"You deserve more."

"I don't. You're all I want," she told him with all the fierceness of her entire soul. "I love you, Dylan. You're mine, and you know what else? I'm yours."

He sucked in a hard breath and she realized he was shaking. Shaking with the effort to not kiss her again. Her hands came up to his chest and she fisted her fingers in his shirt, longing, longing. . . for more.

But it wasn't going to come because he gently wrapped his fingers around her wrists and brought her hands down and stepped back. "'Night, Tee."

"'Night," she whispered. Dammit. She took longer going home, dragging it out another good ten minutes, in spite of everything smiling to herself the whole time.

He'd finally kissed her! It had been a life-changing kiss, the kiss of all kisses, and no matter what he said, there'd be more.

Because he loved her too.

She knew that now, and because she did, she could wait for the rest.

ON MONDAY, DYLAN got to the college campus early, and thanks to his text, so had the other students. They met in the parking lot around his truck and bent their heads over the set of plans he'd printed out.

"Oh my God."

"Wow."

"It's perfect."

The low murmurs gave him a surge of hope. "Yeah?" he asked.

Everyone agreed wholeheartedly that he'd knocked it out of the park. "Okay," he said. "So we're all clear on our roles there." He rolled up the plans and stuffed them back into the toolbox in his truck bed just as a voice spoke from behind him.

"What's going on?"

Everyone turned and looked at Tilly with horrified blank faces. Shit. Dylan shifted, blocking the back of his truck. "We're working hard on our projects," he said.

"You are?" Her brow was furrowed in confusion. "Together?"

He stepped toward her, nudging her aside so no one could hear them. "We're stronger together," he said and watched her look at him speculatively.

"Are we still talking about the project?" she asked. "Or us?"

"In this case, it's a little of both."

She looked past him to the other students. Dylan thought that not one in the bunch would make a good actor—they were all bright eyed and looking like they were holding a big secret.

Which of course they were.

"Look at them," she whispered and he started to grimace until she finished her sentence. "They're excited and inspired."

She sounded so touched that he leaned in to brush a kiss to her temple. "They *are* excited and inspired," he said. "By you. You're doing something really great here, Tee. I hope you know that."

She let out a breath. "Thank you for saying that, but—"

"It's true."

The bell rang. Saved, he thought as everyone headed into class.

The rest of the week went quick. He spent his days working his ass off and his nights seducing Tilly. Best. Week. Ever.

On Friday, he ran from class to work, had several flights and a meeting with Penn and Ric, always with their financial advisor and attorney.

They weren't yet in the black, but they were ahead of projections to be there by the end of the year. Penn and Ric wanted to celebrate, but he shook his head.

"Tilly's show is tonight at the gallery," he said. "You're both going."

"Told you he was in over his head," Penn said to Ric.

Ric nodded. "And it's about time."

Dylan opened his mouth, but Ric kept talking. "And we wouldn't miss the show."

"Wine, cheese, women . . ." Penn smiled innocently. "Sounds like a great time."

Dylan pointed at him. "Don't even think about picking anyone up there tonight."

"Got it," Penn said. "But if they pick me up, that's okay, right?"

Dylan got to the gallery early, wanting to help Tilly set up or just to be moral support. But found Quinn in the parking lot struggling to hoist herself out of her car. He gave her a hand. Actually two hands, and then shook his head when she straightened, a little breathless. "You shouldn't be driving."

"I'm still a week away from delivery," she panted.

"Are you sure?"

She rolled her eyes. "I've gone to the hospital twice with false labor. I'm not going to embarrass myself again. This baby's going to be halfway out before I go back."

He winced at the image. "Where's Mick?"

"He had to run up to San Francisco for a client. He'll be back before the show's over so he can support Tilly."

He led her inside and directly to a chair. Tilly rushed over from the back and dropped to her knees before Quinn. "What is it? Are you okay?"

"I'm fine, the baby's fine! Your boyfriend's just over-protective."

Tilly looked up at Dylan and he did his best to indeed look like a guy she might want as her boyfriend, as juvenile as the word sounded. Because he wanted a whole lot more than to be just her boyfriend. He wanted things he hadn't been able to imagine wanting . . .

"I'm fine," Quinn repeated and shooed the both of them away. "Go. Go enjoy your show. You look amazing."

Tilly accepted Dylan's hand and let him pull her upright. She tugged at the hem of her sexy little black dress that sparkled when she shifted, the material both clingy and yet somehow playing coy with her curves.

"You look beautiful," he said. Actually she was eye-popping and heart-stopping and he wanted to say so, but Quinn was leaning forward to hear their every word and he didn't want her to fall out of the chair.

Tilly smiled up at him, her gaze on his mouth. She wanted a kiss and he wanted to give her one. He turned her away from Quinn and leaned in. "That's some dress," he whispered, his lips ghosting hers.

She smiled and closed the distance, pressing her mouth to his. "Wore it for you," she whispered back. "And to distract myself. I'm so nervous."

"Don't be." He let his gaze move around the room, at the dizzying, colorful array of her art, which was just as eye-popping and heart-stopping as the woman. "It's amazing." He smiled down at her. "Like you."

"You have to say that," she said. "Because you're hoping to get me naked later."

Guilty. He was indeed hoping to get her naked later.

"What if no one comes?" she asked.

He took her hand and pulled her around the corner where she could see into the front room, which was packed.

"Oh my God." She shook a disbelieving head. "Do you think Quinn paid them all to show up?"

"No one's being paid to be here," he said, pulling her out into the room, where one of the gallery owners was walking around with a tray of wineglasses and some hors d'oeuvres. Tilly took two glasses of wine and handed one to Dylan. "I need something for my hands to do," she murmured.

He could think of more than a few ideas, but they weren't suitable for the situation. The hors d'oeuvres weren't exactly the burger and fries he'd have preferred but when Tilly handed him something that looked like a stuffed mushroom, he took it and kept his grimace to himself. On a normal day, he'd rather go back to war than eat a mushroom.

A few more of Tilly's students immediately moved toward her to gush over her work and one said, "I wanted to tell you how much it's meant to me to learn from someone like you, who trusted herself enough to follow her heart."

Tilly looked flustered. And honored.

Dylan took a sip of wine—while wishing it was a beer—and stuffed another of the hors d'oeuvres into his mouth to keep from talking. The students were doing a great job of boosting Tilly's confidence and he didn't want to stop them. She deserved this. And more.

He was going to try to give her that more.

FLUSH FROM ALL the sweet compliments, Tilly looked around the room and saw that many of her works had discreet red stickers on the plaques next to each piece, meaning they'd been sold.

It was an incredibly surreal moment.

But more moving had been the visceral reaction of her students. Deep down, she'd known she was competent at what she did. But she hadn't known that she would make a good teacher, and hadn't known it would matter. She turned in a slow circle, taking it all in, and stopped when she found Dylan watching her.

She smiled. "I thought I'd let myself down, but then you came along and saw me as a better version of myself."

"Then see yourself through my eyes, Tee. You haven't let yourself—or anyone—down."

"And vice versa," she told him, reaching for his hand. "Maybe neither of us turned out how we expected, but . . ." She lifted a shoulder and bumped it to his. "We did all right for a couple of street rats, didn't we?"

He squeezed her hand, his eyes lit with affection and love. God, so much love. "Yeah, we did do pretty good. I've got something I want to do with you."

She leaned in. "Does it involve getting out of this dress? Cuz I ate too many hors d'oeuvres and it's too tight."

His eyes were hot as he slid a hand around the nape of her neck and drew her in close to nuzzle at the sweet spot just beneath her ear. "That first. And then tomorrow morning, I take you away for the weekend to celebrate."

She lifted her face to his. "What are we celebrating?"

"Your success."

"And your new business venture," she said.

"And that," he agreed. "And us."

Biting her lower lip, she knew she didn't even have to think about it. She nodded. And an hour later when he brought her home, Leo greeted her with great enthusiasm, running in madman circles around her feet, yipping, letting her know that he felt she'd been gone way over their agreed upon limit.

When Dylan stepped inside behind her, Leo stopped

to give him a sideways stink eye and actually huffed out a sigh that made her laugh. "He's warming up to you."

Man and dog stared at each other in a standoff, neither looking thrilled.

Dylan took a few steps inside and Leo did what Leo did best. He clamped onto the back of Dylan's pants leg and tried to prevent him from getting any closer to Tilly.

Dylan didn't exhibit any annoyance or frustration. He merely crouched down before the dog. "Look, man," he said. "We both love our girl, right?"

Leo stopped growling.

"Right," Dylan said. "So I don't know what your plans are, but I'm just going to remind you that I saw her first. And I'm happy to share her with you, though that offer's for you and only you. It's a good deal, I'd take it if I was you. Think about it."

Unbearably moved by his kindness to her silly dog, Tilly felt her throat grow tight. Maybe it'd been the show and the emotions it had evoked. And having Dylan fit so effortlessly into her life like he'd never left. Maybe it was all of it, everything, including the sensation of being so happy that it scared her.

God knew she wasn't used to that feeling . . .

She turned away to gather herself and dropped her wrap and purse to the couch. Then she grabbed the bottle of wine she'd taken from the gallery and poured them each a glass to give her something to do with her hands.

What happened now? she wondered. Could they

keep this momentum going and really make something work between them? Was she grown up enough to finally handle him and all the demands a relationship would put on her?

Yes. She knew she could. The question was, could he?

Dylan took her glass and set it aside, leaning into her with another soft kiss. "You're thinking so hard that I smell something burning," he said.

She gnawed on her lower lip. It was true. She had a question. Except the last time she'd asked something close to it, she hadn't gotten an answer out of him. Granted, that had been a lot of years ago . . .

Dylan waited her out, gently teasing her lips with his and the rest of her by just being as close as he was. She could feel the warmth of him, the strength in his leanly muscled body pressing into hers.

"Tee."

He wanted her to put words to her thoughts, something she'd never found easy to do with him right in front of her. She took a deep breath. "Suppose for some reason that you decide not to do this anymore."

"This . . . ?"

"Us."

He looked at her, his deep dark eyes holding hers with an intensity that made breathing all but impossible. He stroked a stray strand of her hair from her forehead. "Tee, I love you. Deciding not to do us would be like me deciding to stop sucking air into my lungs. Not going to happen."

The tightness in her chest eased and she felt a warm glow slide into its place. Her throat tightened as well, and her eyes felt misty. "I love you," she said.

He went utterly still for a beat, his eyes going nearly black. "Yeah?"

"Yeah." She drew in another deep breath, shocked to find she hadn't choked on the words. "And to be honest, I think I always have—" Before she could finish that sentence, he yanked her into him and kissed her.

And kissed her.

She let it all wash over her, the feel of him this close, the way he was holding her as if she was his entire life, and her heart took over the rulership from her brain. She pressed closer still, apparently needing to climb him like a tree. She had a fistful of his hair in one hand and his shirt in the other. "Off," she muttered against his mouth, desperate for the feel of his bare skin to hers.

He broke the kiss long enough to yank his shirt over his head and toss it aside. He had all the strength and muscle, but he didn't take the lead from her, instead leaving her in the driver's seat. She unbuttoned his pants and he shucked them off and stood there wearing nothing but his birthday suit and a half smile as he watched her take in the sight of him.

She did her best not to drool, but the truth was she never had been able to get over how beautiful he was, then or now. Although there was something to the life he'd led that had turned a rough and tumble teenager into a badass man that was drop dead sexy. He knew who and what he was and he made no apology for it.

And he loved her.

She took his hand and led him into the bedroom. Nudged him until he sat on the edge of the bed. Standing between his spread legs, she began to pull off her dress. He put his hands on her waist, helping to guide the material up her body and over her head.

"Pretty," he said of her plain black bra and urged the straps down her arms. When he unhooked it, it slipped away from her body. Leaning in, he kissed a breast. She opened her eyes and met his gaze as his thumbs hooked into her panties and swept them away like everything else.

And still he let her drive. Happy to have the wheel, she climbed into his lap and explored first with her hands and then her mouth. There was little doubt about how much he liked everything she did—he let her know with sexy rough male sounds and caresses that had her own breath catching, but still he didn't take control.

So it was she who climbed over him to reach into his nightstand for a condom. She who drove them both crazy as she slowly rolled it on. She who finally lifted up and brought him inside her. "I love you," she whispered again.

They both began to move then and it was so much more than she'd thought possible. Her heart felt too big for her rib cage, her soul too big for her body. And she could tell by the sounds he made, by how he gripped her, that he felt the same as he met her rhythm. And when they finally tumbled over the edge and got lost in each other, she knew a peace she'd never known before. When she could feel her eyelids again, she lifted them and found him looking at her and she knew he felt the same.

Chapter 9

I've reached that age where my brain goes from
"you probably shouldn't say that" to "what the
hell, let's see what happens."

—from "The Mixed-Up Files of
Tilly Adams's Journal"

Ten years prior:

TILLY CLOSED HER eyes. "Quinn's going to kill me."

"She's not going to kill you," Dylan said calmly.

He was always calm.

She wished she had half his calm. "Yes, she *is* going to kill me. And if for some reason she doesn't, she's going to run to L.A. even faster now, without looking back."

"You stole her car, Tee. You crashed it into a tree and demolished both. I'm not sure what the hell you were thinking, but you must've known you were pretty much saying fuck you when you drove off without her permission, not to mention no driver's license."

Is that what she'd been doing? Trying to push Quinn away before Quinn did it first? Yes. Yes, okay, fine, that's *exactly* what she'd been doing, which made her . . . a child.

Her head was killing her from the cut above her eyebrow, but they said she didn't have a concussion, just a broken arm.

The ER nurse had called her lucky. Tilly laughed bleakly at the thought of being lucky. She hadn't been lucky a single day of her godforsaken life.

Except maybe the day Quinn had come into it . . .

The thought made her want to cry. Luckily she never cried. At least not that she'd admit to. "How did you get so smart?" she asked Dylan.

"The smartest girl I know taught me."

She snorted. "Maybe she's not really all that."

"She is."

She blew out a sigh. "I don't know why I did it. I wanted to stop hurting. I wanted to be somewhere I'm wanted—"

"Tee," Dylan whispered, voice pained.

She shook her head, unable to say anything else.

"You're like her, you know," Dylan said. "Quinn. You're both stubborn. Single-minded." He paused and smiled. "And always sure you're right . . ."

"I don't know why I called you."

". . . beautiful."

She met his warm gaze.

"Courageous," he whispered.

Her throat got tighter.

"Cares about other people like no one else I know," he went on and paused. "I think you got scared because you're afraid to believe in love."

"Well, look who's talking," she managed.

Holding eye contact, he set a hand on either side of her hips and leaned in. "You've been sweet and kind and patient with me, Tilly."

She couldn't tear her eyes from his, so deep and dark and full of the haunting, hollow experiences he'd had in his life, none of which had anything to do with sweet and kind and patient. "It's easy to be those things with you," she said. "I love you, Dylan."

He closed his eyes briefly, as though both pained and moved, and then he looked at her again. "I know you do. And I'm even starting to believe it. I love you too, Tilly."

Completely melted, she lifted her one good arm and set her hand on his biceps. "Dylan—"

"So maybe you can try to be as kind and sweet and patient with Quinn," he said. "Because she's going to barrel in here any second now, frightened, freaked, and half out of her mind."

"How do you know?"

"Because that's how I felt when you called me."

THE NEXT MORNING, Tilly woke up and turned to reach for Dylan, but his side of the bed was cold, indicating that he'd been gone awhile. There was a flash of a memory of him leaning over her in gym clothes for a kiss, reminding her to meet him at ten o'clock on the tarmac for their flight out to their getaway weekend.

He'd gone for a run. She knew his routine now. If they didn't have plans to leave town, he'd have come back for a little more "cardio," where frankly he'd do most of the work because in the early mornings, she was awake enough to be interactive and appreciative, but not enough to take the driver's seat.

The thought made her smile as she got out of bed and into the shower. That had her fully awake enough that she could most definitely take the wheel . . .

She packed and loaded a duffel bag and Leo into the car. Ric had offered to keep the puppy for the weekend, which she was grateful for. Quinn would have done it but she was working very hard at growing a human at the moment and Tilly hadn't wanted to ask her.

She parked at the airport and texted Dylan that she was there. Inside, Ric was at his desk Facetiming with a really cute guy. He came toward Tilly with a smile and took Leo, showing him to the guy on his screen. "This little man is mine all weekend," he said, "so you might want to come by and visit."

The guy on-screen smiled promisingly and they disconnected.

"Are you using my dog as a dude magnet?" Tilly asked.

"Most definitely. Do you mind?"

"Not even a little bit," Tilly said and gave Leo a hug. "Be a good boy and send me Snaps."

She made her way to Dylan's office, but it was dark. In the hallway, she heard the scampering of Leo's paws and turned with a smile as he raced toward her. She scooped him up, waved at Ric who was on the phone again to tell him that she had the pup, and headed back to the open hangar to walk around. Penn had hung pictures on the walls of the guys. In the military. In South America. Here, with some of their clients. There was even one of her and Dylan. She recognized it as being taken that day he'd taken her up for a flight. They'd just gotten off the helicopter and she was grinning wide, hair going crazy in the breeze, looking up at Dylan with an expression of sheer joy.

And love.

It made her suck in a breath. Her body had known it before her brain had.

Dylan was in his leather jacket and dark aviator sunglasses, looking into her face with his mouth curved, and while there was nothing soft about him, the look on his face was most definitely soft.

He loved her back.

It was her own miracle.

But her own miracle was late. She looked at her phone, but nope. No missed call, no text.

Maybe he'd changed his mind, a very small, cruel voice from deep inside her whispered.

After all, he'd done it before . . .

She squeezed Leo for comfort and the pup set his head on her shoulder, his way of giving love. With a sad smile, she turned to go and two arms encircled her from behind.

Dylan.

Relief filling her, she leaned back into him. He nuzzled his jaw to hers, one of his hands coming up to stroke down Leo's back.

The pup froze for a beat and Tilly opened her mouth to warn him not to even think about growling, but Leo didn't. Instead, he leaned up and . . . licked Dylan's jaw before setting his head on Dylan's shoulder.

Dylan smiled as if the affection was simply his due, and Tilly had never loved him more than in that moment.

"Ready?" he asked her.

She started to say yes, but there was something in his voice that she couldn't quite place. Turning in his arms, she looked up at him, but he was wearing an expression she couldn't place either. "I am if you are," she murmured, hoping that her earlier thought of him changing his mind was just paranoia on her part.

He smiled, but seemed distracted as he transferred her duffel bag from her shoulder to his, took Leo back to Ric, and then led them outside.

"Hey," she said softly, dragging her feet until he turned back to look at her. "Is everything okay?"

"Sure." He turned back to the helicopter.

While that small, cruel voice inside her head began to taunt her. *You should freak out now . . .*

But she managed to hold it together and in ten minutes, they were in the air. She loved watching him work the controls like he'd been born to it. Clearly feeling her gaze, he glanced over at her, looking sexy as hell in that headset and dark glasses. He smiled, but it was that odd, distant smile, and her heart congealed.

"It's okay, you know," she said quietly. She didn't have to speak louder, he could hear her in his headset.

Again he glanced at her, his own gaze hidden behind those dark lenses. "What's okay?"

"If you've changed your mind about me. About us."

His expression went completely blank and he turned his attention back to controlling the flight for a painfully long moment. "Why would you think I've changed my mind?" he finally asked.

"Because you're acting weird."

"I'm acting weird?"

"Yes!" she said. "Are you going to tell me what's going on, or just keep repeating whatever I've said?"

He said absolutely nothing to this and she opened her mouth to press for more information than that, but he pointed a finger to his headset, indicating he was listening to something or someone and needed a moment.

Wow. Okay then. So she'd been right and the way her gut had sunk all the way to her toes made her want to throw up. Since he was busy speaking into his headset to someone she couldn't hear in hers, she tuned him out and in order to not cry, she took in the gorgeous view as they headed west from the airport.

It should have taken her breath, but her breath had

already been taken. She pressed her nose to the glass, trying to distract herself by playing the game in her head of placing landmarks. There was downtown. The café. Her house. The highway as they turned and headed toward the ocean. She pressed even closer to the window, wanting to see if she could see the billboard her students were designing and she sucked in a breath because she could indeed see it.

Only there was something on it. A graphic design in bright primary colors with words blocked out . . .

T . . .

Will . . .

You . . .

Marry . . .

Me . . .

Her heart started pounding heavily in her headset, *boom, boom, boom*, so that she couldn't hear anything but the blood whooshing through her veins. Because the billboard appeared to be proof that he hadn't planned on walking away from her at all . . . "Dylan," she whispered, unable to tear her gaze off the words. "What—"

The helicopter jerked as they abruptly changed directions and she lost sight of the billboard. She gripped the dashboard and twisted to look at Dylan. "What—"

"Hold on." His face was still carefully blank as he worked the controls. "We're going back."

Because she'd taken what she now realized had been his nerves as him no longer wanting to be with her. She was an idiot. "Dylan—"

"Your sister's in labor and needs you."

She sucked in a breath. "Is something wrong?"

He didn't answer, just concentrated on flying them back.

"Dylan—"

"Mick called and got Penn. Said we needed to get to the hospital right away."

"Hurry," she whispered.

"Roger that."

Thirty minutes later, they were on the ground and racing toward the hospital in his truck. She was filled with fear and panic.

Still concentrating on the road, Dylan reached over and squeezed her hand. "It'll be okay."

"You don't know that," she whispered, her throat thick with tears.

They hit the maternity ward at a dead run and Tilly grabbed onto the counter like it was a lifeline. "Quinn Hennessey," she managed. "She's in labor and—"

"You Tilly?" the nurse asked, standing up.

"Yes."

"Finally." The nurse took her at a brisk near run down the hallway and shoved a pair of scrubs at her. "Quickly now," the nurse said and then had Tilly wash up before leading her into a labor and delivery room.

Quinn was in the bed, hunched over her bent knees, huffing and puffing like a locomotive. Mick was at her side. A doctor was telling Quinn to keep breathing.

Both Mick and the doctor looked beat to hell.

"I *am* breathing!" Quinn yelled. "And the next person to tell me to keep breathing is going to die!" She caught sight of Tilly in the doorway. "Took you long enough! Get over here and hold my damn hand. I needed to push an hour ago!"

"Why didn't you?"

"I'm not doing this without you!" Quinn huffed and puffed and grabbed onto Quinn's hand with superhuman force, threatening bones and ligaments. "I'm sorry. I know I'm yelling but I can't stop! Mick, get down there with the doctor to catch this baby because she's coming in hot!"

Tilly brought Quinn's hand to her chest and squeezed. "You're okay?"

"Hell, no, I'm not okay. I'm about to push a bowling ball out my hoo-ha!" she yelled, and then she began pushing.

Chapter 10

Dear Heart, please stop getting involved in everything. Your job is to pump blood, that's it.

—from "The Mixed-Up Files of
Tilly Adams's Journal"

AN HOUR LATER Tilly was sitting in the chair beside Quinn's bed, holding the newborn with marvel and more emotion that she wanted to admit to. "Baby Ashlyn," she whispered. "Wow. I can't believe you're here."

And then she burst into tears.

Quinn looked at Mick, who was on the bed with his wife, holding her against him.

Mick got out of the bed, bent to kiss his wife, and left them alone.

"What's up?" Quinn asked.

"She's just so beautiful," Tilly sobbed.

"She's patchy and blotchy and bald," Quinn said. "Now tell me what's wrong."

Tilly laughed in horror at Quinn's description. "She's your baby."

"And I love her more than I can say, but she's not why you're crying like your heart's broken."

"I think I blew it with Dylan," she managed.

"You couldn't possibly. He loves you, ridiculously."

"I misread some cues." Tilly drew a deep breath and tried to get ahold of herself. "I assumed he was going to take off again, only it was the opposite."

"Are you speaking in English?" Quinn asked. "I was in labor for twelve hours and haven't slept in over twenty-four. I'm also starving and sitting on a blown-up dough-nut. So you've got to cut right to the chase for me."

"She's trying to tell you that I'd planned a proposal, which she somehow took for me dumping her," Dylan said from the doorway.

Tilly's heart stopped at the sight of him. So far today, she'd panicked on him, assumed the worst, let him get her here, and then ditched him without a backward glance.

He didn't look mad though.

He glanced at Quinn in question and was nodded in. He moved straight to Tilly and looked down at the baby with a warm, genuine smile that softened the features of his face.

"Do you want to hold her?" Tilly asked and when Dylan nodded, she rose and gently set the baby into his very capable arms.

Dylan bent low and said something soft and inaudible to the baby and then gently handed her back to Quinn. "I need to borrow your sister a moment, do you mind?"

"Does it have anything to do with the ten proposals we've had in town since you put up the billboard?" Mick asked, coming back into the room, slipping his phone into his pocket.

"What?" Tilly asked in shock.

"Yeah." Mick sent Dylan a head shake and a low laugh. "Do you have any idea how many T's live in Wildstone?"

Dylan stared at him for a beat and then laughed. "Sorry. I didn't expect it to go down like that."

Mick glanced over at Tilly. "I'm guessing no one did."

"Someone needs to tell me what the hell's going on," Quinn said. "Because I can go back to yelling. Don't think I won't!"

"I've got this," Mick said to Dylan, referring to Quinn and the baby. "If you want some privacy—"

"No privacy!" Quinn yelled, her voice a little hoarse. "I just pushed this baby out my hoo-ha—"

"Please," Tilly said, slapping her hands to her ears. "I'm begging you, *stop saying that!*"

"I'll stop saying it when you and Dylan stand right here at my bedside and figure your shit out."

Tilly started to shake her head but Dylan came close and took her hand. "I'm willing," he said.

"You're my favorite," Quinn told him. "Keep talking."

Dylan drew a deep breath and met Tilly's gaze. "I had plans for today. Plans that went awry."

There were a lot of words about to escape her, but she felt a little too fragile and exposed so she squeezed her lips together and nodded.

He nodded back and paused, clearly thinking she'd want to speak. When she didn't, he let out a low, mirthless laugh. "Still me. Okay." He drew a breath. "You thought it was over?"

"I . . ." She broke off and bit her lower lip.

"You did," he said, clearly shocked. "You really thought it was over, that I'd changed my mind about you, but that I'd still take you up in the air to what . . . be a dick?"

She bit her lower lip.

He gave a disbelieving head shake. "You did. You actually believed that in the hours since I'd worshipped every single inch of your body that I'd somehow decided to walk away, that it was over."

She closed her eyes. "In my defense, that is what happened last time."

"Tilly," Quinn whispered, horrified.

Dylan just inhaled a deep breath and let it out slow and controlled. "It *is* what happened last time. But it was a long time ago," he said with quiet steel. "I was a stupid, reckless kid who had no idea how to hold on to what had turned out to be the very best thing in his entire life."

"Oh," Quinn breathed and used Mick's shirt to blot her tears. "Don't mind me. It's baby hormones."

Tilly's eyes had filled too and she didn't have baby hormones to blame.

Dylan pulled her into him. "Let me start over," he said. "This is long haul stuff. Clearly, I'm not perfect. I'm going to mess up—"

"Well, you're not alone there," she managed.

A very small smile curved his lips. "Good to know. But I'm never going to leave you again. Ever."

As he said it, she felt her heart click back into place as the reality washed over her. He was real, they were real, and neither of them were going anywhere.

Dylan dropped to a knee in front of her.

Quinn gasped and burst into tears. "I'm sorry! Ignore me! Carry on!"

There was a small smile on Dylan's mouth as he looked up at Tilly. "We were supposed to be hovering in front of the billboard for this, but life with you is never going to be that predictable, is it?"

She gave a shake of her head. "I don't think it will be," she whispered. "Are you really asking me to marry you?"

"I'm trying." He pulled a little black box from his pocket.

Before she could say another word, she dropped to her knees too. Mostly because hers didn't want to hold her up anymore. "*Yes.*"

"But he didn't ask yet!" Quinn said.

"Shh," Mick told Quinn very gently and then kissed her, probably to ensure she'd stay zipped.

"Yes," Tilly said again, in case Dylan hadn't heard.

He smiled. "I had a speech all prepared in my head."

"Does it go something like 'I love you, I've always loved you, and I'll never love anyone other than you'?" Tilly asked, throwing her arms around him. "Because that's how I feel about you. I messed up your first proposal—"

"Actually, technically," Mick said helpfully from the bed above them. "That was my wife who messed it up."

"My point," Tilly said, ignoring their audience, her voice shaking but her heart steady for the first time all day. "--Is that the least I can do is ask you. Dylan . . ." She smiled through her tears. "You're it for me. And I'm it for you. Will you marry me?"

He grinned. "Yes," he said and kissed her to seal the deal just as baby Ashlyn began to wail.

"Do you think Tilly meant it when she said she'd babysit any time?" Tilly heard her sister ask Mick. "Because now would be good."

"I've got you," Mick told Quinn and Tilly assumed he took the baby because she stopped crying. Which was good because Tilly would do anything for Ashlyn, anything but take her lips off Dylan's anytime soon.

**Keep reading for a peek at Jill Shalvis's
next full-length women's fiction novel**

RAINY DAY FRIENDS

Six months after Lanie Jacobs' husband death,
it's hard to imagine anything could deepen
her sense of pain and loss. But then Lanie
discovers she isn't the only one grieving his
sudden passing. A serial adulterer, he left
behind several other women who, like Lanie,
each believe she was his legally wedded wife.

Rocked by the infidelity, Lanie is left to grapple
with searing questions. How could she be so
wrong about a man she thought she knew better
than anyone? Will she ever be able to trust
another person? Can she even trust herself?

Desperate to make a fresh start, Lanie impulsively takes
a job at the family-run Capriotti Winery. At first, she
feels like an outsider among the boisterous Capriottis.
With no real family of her own, she's bewildered by how

quickly they all take her under their wing and make her feel like she belongs. Especially Mark Capriotti, a gruffly handsome Air Force veteran turned deputy sheriff who manages to wind his way into Lanie's cold, broken heart—along with the rest of the clan.

Everything is finally going well for her, but the arrival of River Brown changes all that. The fresh-faced twenty-one-year old seems as sweet as they come . . . until her dark secrets come to light—secrets that could destroy the new life Lanie's only just begun to build.

On Sale June 2018!

ANXIETY GIRL, ABLE to jump to the worst conclusion in a single bound!

Most of the time karma was a bitch, but every once in a while she could be surprisingly nice, even kind. Lanie Jacobs, way past overdue for both of those things, told herself this was her time. Seize the day and all that. She drew a deep breath as she exited the highway at Wildstone.

The old Wild West California town was nestled in the rolling hills between the Pacific Coast and wine and ranching country. She'd actually grown up not too far from here, though it felt like a lifetime ago. The road was narrow and curvy, and since it'd rained earlier, she added tricky and slick to her growing list of its issues. She was already white-knuckling a sharp turn when a kamikaze squirrel darted into her lane, causing her to nearly swerve into oncoming traffic before remembering the rules of country driving.

Never leave your lane; not for weather, animals, or even God himself.

Luckily the squirrel reversed its direction, but before Lanie could relax a trio of deer bounded out right in front of her. "Run, Bambi, run," she cried, hitting the brakes, and by the skin of all of their collective teeth, they missed one another.

Sweating, nerves sizzling like live wires, she finally turned onto Capriotti Lane and parked as she'd been instructed.

And went completely still as her world darkened. Not physically, but internally as her entire body braced for all hell to break loose. Recognizing sign número uno of an impending anxiety attack barreling down on her like a freight train, she gripped the steering wheel. "You're okay," she told herself firmly.

This, of course, didn't stop said freight train. But though she'd been plagued with overactive fight-or-flight preceptors, all of which were yelling at her to run, she couldn't.

Wouldn't.

Not this time. Which didn't stop the dizziness or sudden nausea, or make her lungs work properly. And that was the hardest thing about these attacks that were new to her this year, because it was always the same fears. What if it never stopped? What if someone saw her losing it and realized she was broken? And the worst part . . . what if it wasn't an anxiety attack? Maybe this time it was a seizure or a brain aneurism.

Or a stroke. Hadn't her great-aunt Agnes died of a stroke?

Okay, stop, she ordered herself, damp with sweat now and doing that annoying trembling thing where she shook like a leaf. *Breathe in for four, breathe out for four, and hold for four.*

Repeat.

Repeat again, all while listing the meals she'd had

yesterday in her head. Peanut butter toast for breakfast. Tuna salad for lunch. She'd skipped dinner and had wine and popcorn instead.

Slowly but surely, her pulse slowed. *It's all good,* she told herself, but because she wasn't buying what she was selling, she had to force herself out of the car like she was a five-year-old starting kindergarten instead of being thirty and simply facing a brand-new job. Given all she'd been through, this should be easy, even fun. But sometimes adulthood felt like the vet's office and she was the dog excited for the car ride—only to find out the destination.

Shaking her head, she strode across the parking lot. It was April, which meant the rolling hills to the east were green and lush and the Pacific Ocean to the west looked like a surfer's dream, all of it so gorgeous it could've been a postcard. A beautiful smoke screen over her not-so-beautiful past. The air was scented like a really expensive sea-and-earth candle, though all Lanie could smell was her forgotten hopes and dreams. With wood chips crunching under her shoes, she headed through the entrance, beneath which was a huge wooden sign that read:

CAPRIOTTI WINERY,
FROM OUR FIELDS TO YOUR
TABLE . . .

Her heart sped up. Nerves, of course, the bane of her existence. But after a very crappy few years, she was changing her path. For once in her godforsaken life, something was going to work out for her. *This* was going to work out for her.

She was grimly determined.

The land was lined with split-rail wooden fencing, protecting grapevines as far as the eye could see. The large open area in front of her was home to several barns and other structures, all meticulously maintained and landscaped with stacks of barrels, colorful flower beds, and clever glass bottle displays.

Lanie walked into the first "barn," which housed the reception area and offices for the winery. She was greeted by an empty reception counter, beyond which was a huge, open-beamed room containing a bar on the far side, comfy couches and low tables scattered through the main area, and walls of windows that showed off the gorgeous countryside.

It was warm and inviting and . . . empty. Well, except for the huge mountain of white and gray fur sleeping on a dog bed in a corner. It was either a Wookie or a massive English sheepdog, complete with scraggly fur hanging in its eyes. If it was a dog, it was the hugest one she'd ever seen, and she froze as the thing snorted, lifted its head, and opened a bleary eye.

At the sight of her, it leapt to its four paws and gave a happy *"wuff!"* At least she was hoping it was a happy *wuff* because it came running at her. Never having owned a dog in her life, she froze. "Uh, hi," she said, and did her best to hold her ground. But the closer the thing got, the more she lost her nerve. She whirled to run.

And then she heard a crash.

She turned back in time to see that the dog's forward momentum had been too much. Its hind end had come out from beneath it and it'd flipped onto its back, skidding to a stop in front of her.

She—because she was definitely a she, Lanie could now see—flopped around like a fish for a few seconds as she tried to right herself, to no success. With a loud woof, the dog gave up and stayed on her back, tail wagging like crazy, tongue lolling out of the side of her mouth.

"You're vicious, I see," Lanie said, and unable to resist, she squatted down to rub the dog's belly.

The dog snorted her pleasure, licked her hand, and then lumbered up and back over to her bed.

Lanie looked around. Still alone. Eleven forty-five. She was fifteen minutes early, which was a statement on her entire life.

You'll be the only human to ever be early for her own funeral, her mom liked to say, along with her favorite— *you expect way too much out of people.*

This from the woman who'd been a physicist and who'd regularly forgotten to pick up her own daughter after school.

Lanie eyed the sign on the reception desk and realized the problem. The winery was closed on Mondays and Tuesdays, and today was Monday. "Hello?" she called out, feeling a little panicky. Had she somehow screwed up the dates? She'd interviewed for a two-month graphic artist job here twice, both times via Skype from her Santa Barbara apartment. Her new boss, Cora Capriotti, the winery office manager, wanted her to create new labels, menus, a website, everything, and she wanted her to do so on-site. Cora had explained that they prided themselves on being old-fashioned. It was part of their charm, she'd said.

Lanie didn't mind the temporary relocation from Santa Barbara, two hours south of here. She'd actually quit her permanent graphic design job after her husband's death. Needing a big change and a kick in her own ass to get over herself and all the self-pity, she'd been freelancing ever since. It'd been good for her. She'd accepted this job specifically because it was in Wildstone. Far enough away from Santa Barbara to give her a sense of a new start . . . and an excuse to go back to her roots. She'd grown up only fifteen minutes from here and she'd secretly hoped that maybe she and her mom might spend some time together in the same room. In any case, two months away from her life was exactly what the doctor had ordered.

Literally.

She pulled out her cell phone, scrolled for her new boss's number, and called.

"We're out back!" Cora answered. "Let yourself in and join us for lunch!"

"Oh, but I don't want to interrupt—" Lanie blinked and stared at her phone.

Cora had disconnected.

With another deep breath that was long on nerves and short on actual air, she walked through the open great room and out the back French double doors. She stepped onto a patio beautifully decorated with strings of white lights and green foliage lining the picnic-style tables. But that wasn't what had her frozen like a deer facing down the headlights of a speeding Mack Truck.

No, that honor went to the people crowded around two of the large tables, which had been pushed close together. Everyone turned to look at her in unison, all ages and sizes, and then started talking at once.

Lanie recognized that they were smiling and waving, which meant they were probably a friendly crowd, but parties weren't her friends. Her favorite party trick was *not* going to parties.

A woman in her early fifties broke away. She had dark brunette hair liberally streaked with gray, striking dark brown eyes, and a kind smile. She was holding a glass of red wine in one hand and a delicious-looking hunk of bread in the other, and she waved both in Lanie's direction.

"Lanie, right? I'm Cora, come on in."

Lanie didn't move. "I've caught you in the middle of something. A wedding or a party. I can come back—"

"Oh, no, it's nothing like that." Cora looked back at the wild pack of people still watching. "It's just lunch. We do this every day." She gestured at all of them. "Meet your fellow employees. I'm related to everyone one way or another, so they'll behave. Or else." She smiled, taking away the heat of the threat. "In any case, welcome. Come join us. Let me get you a plate—"

"Oh, that's okay, I brought a sandwich." Lanie patted

her bag. "I can just go sit in my car until you're finished—"

"No need for that, honey. I have lunch catered every day."

"Every day?" She didn't realize she'd spoken out loud until Cora laughed.

"It's our social time," Cora said.

At Lanie's last job, people had raced out of the building at lunch to escape one another. "That's . . . very generous of you."

"Nothing generous about it," Cora said with a laugh. "It keeps everyone on-site, ensures no one's late getting back to the job, and I get to keep my nosy nose in everyone's business." She set aside her bread, freeing up a hand to grab Lanie's, clearly recognizing a flight risk when she saw one. "Everyone," she called out. "This is Lanie Jacobs, our new graphic artist." She smiled reassuringly at Lanie and gestured to the group of people. "Lanie, this is everyone; from the winemaker to the front-desk receptionist, we're all here. We're a rather informal bunch."

They all burst into applause, and Lanie wished for a big black hole to sink into and vanish. "Hi," she managed, and gave a little wave. She must have pulled off the correct level of civility because they all went back to eating and drinking wine, talking among themselves.

"Are you really related to all of them?" she asked Cora, watching two little girls, possibly twins, given their matching toothless smiles, happily eating chocolate cupcakes, half of which were all over their faces.

Cora laughed. "Just about. I've got a big family. You?"

"No."

"Single?"

"Yes." Lanie's current relationship status: *sleeping diagonally across her bed.*

Cora smiled. "Well, I'll be happy to share my people—there's certainly enough of us to go around. Hey," she yelled, cupping a hand around her mouth. "Someone take the girls in to wash up, and no more cupcakes or they'll be bouncing off the walls."

So the cupcakes were a problem, but wine at lunch wasn't. Good to know.

Cora smiled at Lanie's expression, clearly reading her thoughts. "We're Californians," she said. "We're serious about our wine, but laid-back about everything else. In fact, maybe that should be our tagline. Now come, have a seat." She drew Lanie over to the tables. "We'll get to work soon enough."

There was an impressive amount of food, all of it Italian, all of it fragrant and delicious-looking. Lanie's heart said *definitely* to both the wine and the lasagna, but her pants said *holy shit, woman, find a salad instead.*

Cora gave a nudge to the woman at the end of the table, who looked to be around Lanie's age and had silky dark hair and matching eyes. "Scoot," Cora said.

The woman scooted. So did everyone else, allowing a space on the end for Lanie.

"Sit," Cora told Lanie. "Eat. Make merry."

"But—"

"Oh, and be careful of that one," Cora said, pointing to the woman directly across from Lanie, this one in her early twenties with the same gorgeous dark hair and eyes as the other. "Her bad attitude can be contagious."

"Gee, thanks, Mom," she said with an impressive eye-roll.

Cora blew her daughter a kiss and fluttered away, grabbing a bottle of wine from the middle of one of the tables and refilling glasses as she went.

"One of these days I'm gonna roll my eyes so hard I'm going to go blind," her daughter muttered.

The twins ran through, still giggling, and still looking like they'd bathed in chocolate, which caused a bit of commotion. Trying to remain inconspicuous, Lanie pulled her lunch out of her bag, a homemade salad in a container, sans dressing.

"Are you kidding me?" Cora's daughter asked. "Do you *want* her to come back here and yell at us for not feeding you properly? Put that away." She stood up, reached for a stack of plates in the middle of the table, and handed Lanie one. "Here. Now fill it up and eat, and for God's sake, look happy while you're at it or she'll have my ass."

Lanie eyeballed the casserole dishes lining the center of the tables. Spaghetti, lasagna . . .

"Don't worry, it all tastes as good as it looks," an old man said from the middle of the table. There was no hair on his head, but he did have a large patch of gray steel fuzz on his chest, which was sticking out from the top of his polo shirt. His olive complexion had seen at least seven decades of sun, but his smile was pure little-boy mischief. "And don't worry about your cholesterol either," he added. "I'm seventy-five and I've eaten like this every single day of my life." He leaned across the table and shook her hand. "Leonardo Antony Capriotti. And this is my sweetheart of fifty-four years, Adelina Capriotti. I'd use her middle name, but she refuses to sleep with me when I do that."

The older woman next to him was teeny-tiny, her white hair in a tight bun on her head, her spectacles low on her nose, her smile mischievous. "Gotta keep him in line, you know. Nice to meet you."

Lanie knew from her research on the company that it'd been Leonardo and Adelina who had started this winery back in the seventies, though they'd since handed over the day-to-day reins to their daughter, who Lanie now realized was her boss, Cora. "Nice to meet you both," she said.

"Likewise. You're going to give us a new updated look and make me look good," he said. "Right?"

"Right," she said and hoped that was actually true. No pressure or anything . . .

He smiled. "I like you. Now eat."

If she ate any of this stuff, she'd need a nap by midafternoon. But not wanting to insult anyone, she scooped as little as she felt she could get away with onto her plate and pushed it around with her fork, trying to resist temptation.

"Uh-oh," Cora's daughter said. "We have a dieter."

"Stop it," the woman next to Lanie said. "You'll scare her away and end up right back on Mom's shit list."

Cora's daughter, whose shirt read: LIVE, LAUGH, AND LEAVE ME THE HELL ALONE, snorted. "We both know that I never get *off* the shit list. I just move up and down on it. Mom's impossible to please."

"Don't listen to her," the other woman said to Lanie. "I'm Alyssa, by the way. And Grumpy-Ass over there is my baby sister, Mia."

Mia waved and reached for the breadbasket. "I'm giving up on getting a bikini body, so pass the butter, please. Grandma says the good Lord put alcohol and carbs on this planet for a reason and I'll be damned if I'm going to let Him down."

Her grandma toasted her.

"Mia and I work here at the winery," Alyssa said and gently patted the cloth-wrapped little bundle swaddled to her chest. "This is Elsa, my youngest."

"Elsa, like the princess?" Lanie asked.

"More like the queen," Alyssa said with a smile, rubbing her infant's tush. "She's going to rule this roost someday."

"Who are you kidding?" Mia asked. "Mom's going to hold the reins until she's three hundred years old. That's how long witches live, you know."

Lanie wasn't sure how to react. After all, that witch was now her boss.

"You're scaring her off again," Alyssa said and looked at Lanie. "We love Mom madly, I promise. Mia's just bitchy because she got dumped last night, was late for work this morning, and got read the riot act. She thinks life sucks."

"Yeah well, life *does* suck," Mia said. "It sucks donkey balls. And this whole waking-up-every-morning thing is getting a bit excessive. But Alyssa's right. Don't listen to me. Sarcasm. It's how I hug."

Alyssa reached across the table and squeezed her sister's hand in her own, her eyes soft. "Are you going to tell me what happened? I thought you liked this one."

Mia shrugged. "I was texting him and he was only responding occasionally with 'K.' I mean, I have no idea what 'K' even means. Am I to assume he intended to type 'OK,' but was stabbed and couldn't expend the energy to type an extra whole letter?"

Alyssa sucked her lips into her mouth in a clear attempt not to laugh. "Tell me you didn't ask him that and then get broken up with by text."

"Well, dear know-it-all sister, that's exactly what happened. And now I've got a new motto: *Don't waste your good boob years on a guy that doesn't deserve them.* Oh, and side note: no man does. Men suck."

Lanie let out a completely inadvertent snort of agreement and both women looked over at her.

"Well, they do," she said. "Suck."

"See, I *knew* I was going to like you." Mia reached

for a bottle of red and gestured with it in Lanie's direction.

She shook her head. "Water's good, thanks."

Mia nodded. "I like water too. It solves a lot of problems. Wanna lose weight? Drink water. Tired of your man? Drown him." She paused and cocked her head in thought. "In hindsight, I should've gone *that* route . . ."

A man came out onto the patio, searched the tables, and focused in on Alyssa. He came up behind her, cupped her face, and tilted it up for his kiss. And he wasn't shy about it either, smiling intimately into her eyes first. Running his hands down her arms to cup them around the baby, he pulled back an inch. "How are my girls?" he murmured.

"Jeez, careful or she'll suffocate," Mia said.

"Hmm." The man kissed Alyssa again, longer this time before finally lifting his head. "What a way to go." He turned to Lanie and smiled. "Welcome. I'm Owen Booker, the winemaker."

Alyssa, looking a little dazed, licked her lips. "And husband," she added to his resume. "He's my husband." She beamed. "I somehow managed to land the best winemaker in the country."

Owen laughed softly and borrowed her fork to take a bite of her pasta. "I'll see you at the afternoon meeting," he said, then he bent and brushed a kiss on Elsa's little head and walked off.

Alyssa watched him go. Specifically watched his ass, letting out a theatrical sigh.

"Good God, give it a rest," Mia griped. "And you're drooling. Get yourself together, woman. Yesterday you wanted to kill him, remember?"

"Well, he *is* still a man," Alyssa said. "If I didn't want to kill him at least once a day, he's not doing his job right."

"Please, God, tell me you're almost done with the baby hormonal mood swings," Mia said.

"Hey, I'm hardly having any baby-hormone-related mood swings anymore."

Mia snorted and looked at Lanie. "FYI, whenever we're in a situation where I happen to be the voice of reason, it's probably an apocalypse sort of thing and you should save yourself."

"Whatever," Alyssa said. "He's hot and he's mine, all mine."

"Yes," Mia said. "We know. And he's been yours since the second grade and you get to sleep with him later, so . . ."

Alyssa laughed. "I know. Isn't it great? All you need is love."

"I'm pretty sure we also need water, food, shelter, vodka, and Netflix."

"Well excuse me for being happy." Alyssa looked at Lanie. "Are you married, Lanie?"

"Not anymore." She took a bite of the most amazing fettuccine Alfredo she'd ever had and decided that maybe calories on Mondays didn't count.

"Was he an asshole?" Mia asked, her eyes curious but warmly so.

"Actually, he's dead."

Alyssa gasped. "I'm so sorry. I shouldn't have asked—"

"No," Lanie said, kicking herself for spilling the beans like that. "It's okay. It's been six months." Six months, one week, and two days but hey, who was counting? She bypassed her water and reached for the wine after all. When in Rome . . .

"That's really not very long," Alyssa said.

"I'm really okay." There was a reason for the quick recovery. Several, actually. They'd dated for six months and he'd been charming and charismatic, and new to love, she'd fallen fast. They'd gotten married and gone five years, the first half great, the second half not so much because she'd discovered they just weren't right for each other. She'd not been able to put her finger on what had been wrong exactly, but it'd been undeniable that whatever they'd once shared had faded. But after Kyle had passed away, some things had come to light. Such as the fact that he'd hidden an addiction from her.

A wife addiction.

It'd gone a long way toward getting her over the hump of the grieving process. So had the fact that several other women had come out of the woodwork claiming to also be married to Kyle. Not that she intended to share that humiliation. Not now or ever.

You're my moon and my stars, he'd always told her.

Yeah. Just one lie in a string of many, as it'd turned out . . .

Cora came back around and Lanie nearly leapt up in relief. Work! Work was going to save her.

"I see you've met some of my big, nosy, interfering, boisterous, loving family and survived to tell the tale," Cora said, slipping an arm around Mia and gently squeezing.

"Yes, and I'm all ready to get to it," Lanie said.

"Oh, not yet." Cora gestured for her to stay seated. "No rush, there's still fifteen minutes left of lunch." And then she once again made her way around the tables, chatting with everyone she passed. "Girls," she called out to the cupcake twins, who were now chasing each other around the other table. "Slow down, please!"

At Lanie's table, everyone had gotten deeply involved in a discussion on barrels. She was listening with half an ear to the differences in using American oak versus French oak when a man in a deputy sheriff's uniform came in unnoticed through the French double doors. He was tall, built, and fully armed. His eyes were covered by dark aviator sunglasses, leaving his expression unreadable. And intimidating as hell.

He strode directly toward her.

"Scoot," he said to the table, and since no one else scooted—in fact no one else even looked over at him—Lanie scooted.

"Thanks." He sat, reaching past her to accept the plate that Mia handed to him without pausing her conversation with Alyssa. The plate was filled up to shockingly towering heights that surely no one human could consume.

He caught Lanie staring.

"That's a lot of food," she said inanely.

"Hungry." He grabbed a fork. "You're the new hire."

"Lanie," she said and watched in awe as he began to shovel in food like he hadn't eaten in a week.

"Mark," he said after swallowing a bite, something she appreciated because Kyle used to talk with his mouth full and it had driven her to want to kill him. Which, as it turned out, hadn't been necessary. A heart attack had done that for her.

Apparently cheating on a bunch of wives had been highly stressful. Go figure.

"You must be a very brave woman," Mark said.

And for a horrifying minute, she was afraid she'd spoken of Kyle out loud, and she stared at him.

"Taking on this job, this family," he said. "They're insane, you know. Every last one of them."

Because he had a disarming smile and was speaking with absolutely no malice, she knew he had to be kidding. But she still thought it rude considering they'd served him food. "They can't be all that bad," she said. "They're feeding you, which you seem to be enjoying."

"Who wouldn't enjoy it? It's the best food in the land."

This was actually true. She watched him go at everything on his plate like it was a food-eating contest and he was in danger of coming in second place for the world championship. She shook her head in awe. "You're going to get heartburn eating that fast."

"Better than not eating at all," he said, glancing at his watch. "I've got ten minutes to be back on the road chasing the bad guys, and a lot of long, hungry hours ahead of me."

"One of those days, huh?"

"One of those years," he said. "But at least I'm not stuck here at the winery day in and day out."

It was her turn to go brows up. "Are you making fun of my job at all?"

"Making fun? No," he said. "Offering sympathy, yes. You clearly have no idea what you've gotten yourself into. You could still make a break for it, you know."

That she herself had been thinking the very same thing only five minutes ago didn't help. Suddenly feeling defensive for this job she hadn't even started yet, she looked around her. The winery itself was clearly lovingly and beautifully taken care of. The yard in which they sat was lush and colorful and welcoming. Sure, the sheer number of people employed here was intimidating, as was the fact that they gathered every day to eat lunch and socialize. But she'd get used to it.

Maybe.

"I love my job," she said.

Mark grinned. "You're on day one. And you haven't started yet or you'd have finished your wine. Trust me, it's going to be a rough ride, Lanie Jacobs."

Huh. So he definitely knew more about her than she knew about him. No big deal since she wasn't all that interested in knowing more about him. "Surely given what you do for a living, you realize there's nothing 'rough' about my job at all."

"I know I'd rather face down thugs and gangbangers daily than work in this looney bin."

She knew he was kidding, that he was in fact actually pretty funny, but she refused to be charmed. Fact was, she couldn't have been charmed by any penis-carrying human being at the moment. "Right," she said, "because clearly you're here against your will, being held hostage and force-fed all this amazing food. How awful for you."

"Yeah, life's a bitch." He eyeballed the piece of cheese bread on her plate that she hadn't touched. It was the last one.

She nodded for him to take it and then watched in amazement as he put that away too. "I have to ask," she said. "How in the world do you stay so . . ." She gestured with a hand toward his clearly well-taken-care-of body and struggled with a word to describe him. She supposed *hot* worked—if one was into big, annoying, perfectly fit alphas—not that she intended to say so, since she was pretty sure he knew exactly how good he looked.

"How do I stay so . . . what?" he asked.

"Didn't anyone ever tell you that fishing for compliments is unattractive?"

He surprised her by laughing, clearly completely unconcerned with what she thought of him. "My days tend to burn up a lot of calories," he said.

"Uh-huh."

He pushed his dark sunglasses to the top of his head, and she was leveled with dark eyes dancing with mischievousness. "Such cynicism in one so young."

A plate of cupcakes was passed down the table and Lanie eyed them, feeling her mouth water. She had only so much self-control and apparently she was at her limit because she took one, and then, with barely a pause, she grabbed a second as well. Realizing the deputy sheriff was watching her and looking amused while he was at it, she shrugged. "Sometimes I reward myself before I accomplish something. It's called pre-award motivation."

"Does it work?"

"Absolutely one hundred percent not," she admitted and took a bite of one of the cupcakes, letting out a low moan before she could stop herself. "Oh. My. God."

His eyes darkened to black. "You sound like that cupcake is giving you quite the experience."

She held up a finger for silence, possibly having her first-ever public orgasm.

He leaned in a little bit and since their thighs were already plastered together, he didn't have to go far to speak directly into her ear. "Do you make those same sexy sounds when you—"

She pointed at him again because she still couldn't talk, and he just grinned. "Yeah," he said. "I bet you do. And now I know what I'm going to be thinking about for the rest of the day."

"You'll be too busy catching the bad guys, remember?"

"I'm real good at multitasking," he said.

She let out a laugh, though it was rusty as hell. It'd

been a while since she'd found something funny. Not that this changed her idea of him. He was still too sure of himself, too cocky, and she'd had enough of that to last a lifetime. But she also was good at multitasking and could both not like him and appreciate his sense of humor at the same time.

What she couldn't appreciate was when his smile turned warm and inviting, because for a minute something passed between them, something she couldn't—or didn't—intend to recognize.

"Maybe I could call you sometime," he said.

Before she could turn him down politely, the little cupcake twins came running, leaping at him, one of them yelling, "Daddy, Daddy, Daddy! Look what we got!"

Catching them both with impressive ease, Mark stood, managing to somehow confiscate the cupcakes and set them aside before getting covered in chocolate. "Why is it," he asked Lanie over their twin dark heads, "that when a child wants to show you something, they try to place it directly in your cornea?"

Still completely floored, Lanie could only shake her head.

Mark adjusted the girls so that they hung upside down off his back. This had them erupting in squeals of delight as he turned back to face Lanie again, two little ankles in each of his big hands. "I know what you're thinking," he said into her undoubtedly shocked face. "I think it every day."

Actually, even she had no idea what she was thinking except . . . he was a Capriotti? How had she not seen that coming?

"Yeah," he said. "I'm one of them, which is why I get to bitch about them. And let me guess . . . you just decided you're not going to answer my call?"

Most definitely not, but before she could say so out loud Cora was back, going up on tiptoes to kiss Mark on the cheek. "Hey, baby. Heard you had a real tough night."

He shrugged.

"You get enough to eat?" she asked. "Yes?" She eyed his empty plate and then, with a nod of satisfaction, reached up and ruffled his hair. "Good. But don't for a single minute think, Marcus Antony Edward Capriotti, that I don't know who sneaked your grandpa the cigars he was caught smoking last night."

From his seat at the table, "Grandpa," aka Leonardo Antony Capriotti, lifted his hands as if to say, *Who, me?*

Cora shook her head at both of them, helped the girls down from Mark's broad shoulders, took them by the hand, and walked away.

No, Lanie would most definitely *not* be taking the man's call. And not for the reasons he'd assume either. She didn't mind that he had kids. What she minded was that here was a guy who appeared to have it all: close family, wonderful children, a killer smile, a hot body . . . without a single clue about just how damn lucky he was. It made her mad, actually.

He took in her expression. "Okay, so you're most definitely not going to take my call."

"It's nothing personal," she said. "I just don't date . . ."

"Dads?"

Actually, as a direct result of no longer trusting love, not even one little teeny, tiny bit, she didn't date *anyone* anymore, but that was none of his business.

He looked at her for another beat and whatever lingering amusement he'd retained left him, and he simply nodded as he slid his sunglasses back over his eyes. "Good luck today," he said. "You really are going to need it."

And then he was gone.

He thought she'd judged him. She hated that he thought that, but it was best to let him think it. Certainly better than the truth, which was that the problem was her, all her. She inhaled a deep, shaky breath and turned, surprised to find not just Cora watching, but Mark's sisters, grandpa, and several others she could only guess were also related.

Note to self: *Capriottis multiply when left unattended.*